W9-AOO-777

WHEN
SEA
BECOMES
SKY

Also by Gillian McDunn

WHEN
SEA
BECOMES
SKY

Gillian McDunn

BLOOMSBURY
CHILDREN'S BOOKS

NEW YORK LONDON OXFORD NEW DELHI SYDNEY

BLOOMSBURY CHILDREN'S BOOKS
Bloomsbury Publishing Inc., part of Bloomsbury Publishing Plc
1385 Broadway, New York, NY 10018

BLOOMSBURY, BLOOMSBURY CHILDREN'S BOOKS,
and the Diana logo are trademarks of Bloomsbury Publishing Plc

First published in the United States of America in February 2023
by Bloomsbury Children's Books

Bloomsbury books may be purchased for business or promotional use.
For information on bulk purchases please contact Macmillan Corporate and
Premium Sales Department at specialmarkets@macmillan.com

Library of Congress Cataloging-in-Publication Data
Names: McDunn, Gillian, author.
Title: When sea becomes sky / by Gillian McDunn.
Description: New York: Bloomsbury Children's Books, [2023]
Summary: As Pelican Island's history-making drought wears on,
the water level on Bex and Davey's beloved marsh reveals
the hand of a statue that has been underneath the water for who knows
how long, and the siblings are determined to find out more.
Identifiers: LCCN 2022021616 (print) | LCCN 2022021617 (e-book)
ISBN 978-1-5476-1085-3 (hardcover) • ISBN 978-1-5476-1086-0 (e-book)
Subjects: CYAC: Brothers and sisters—Fiction. | Droughts—fiction. |
Statues—Fiction. | LCGFT: Novels.
Classification: LCC PZ7.1.M43453 Wh 2023 (print) | LCC PZ7.1.M43453
(e-book) | DDC [Fic]—dc23
LC record available at https://lccn.loc.gov/2022021616

Book design by Jeanette Levy
Typeset by Westchester Publishing Services
Printed and bound in the U.S.A.
2 4 6 8 10 9 7 5 3 1

To find out more about our authors and books visit
www.bloomsbury.com and sign up for our newsletters.

For Andy and Jared,
forever my brothers

WHEN SEA BECOMES SKY

PART ONE

313 days without rain

CHAPTER 1

Some summers are the funnest and some summers are the longest but last summer was perfectly ordinary until the day we found the hand.

Well, not *exactly* ordinary. Let me back up and start again.

On the day we found the hand, it hadn't rained for almost an entire year. It wasn't a dry spell—it was a real, official drought that showed no signs of stopping.

I'd never thought twice about the rain until it disappeared on us, but that summer I had a constant crick in my neck from staring upward, wondering what might come next.

I wasn't the only one.

"Bex," my usually patient little brother, Davey, would say, sighing deeply. "Is it *ever* going to rain?"

I didn't know how to answer. For everyone on our island, weather had become a never-ending topic of conversation. Once in a while we'd get our hopes up, if a breeze was cool or if the air had a certain heaviness. But day after day passed without a single drop.

There was an itchiness we felt, like we were waiting for something big to happen. On Pelican Island, June clouds should be fat cotton balls, bursting with afternoon thunderstorms that rattle your teeth. But that summer, the sky was pale and eerily still. The grass was dry and crunchy. Even the dirt looked thirsty.

Besides the weather, a few other things made the summer unusual. Dad pulled double shifts on the ferryboat, Mom seemed tired all the time, and Davey had stopped speaking to anyone but me. But except for that, you could say it was a regular kind of summer. At least, it *was*—until the day I saw something poking up above the water and decided to investigate. That was when it officially became the Summer of the Hand.

Officially, anyway, to Davey and me, which was really all that mattered.

So I guess that's where I'll start.

CHAPTER 2

Over the worn edges of my black composition book, I peeked at Davey. He was reading, propped up on his skinny elbows and sprawled across an especially wide branch of the big live oak we climbed most afternoons.

We were in our special place, which was called The Thumb—named for the way the far corner of our island curved back toward the mainland, like it was trying to hitch a ride to shore. When we were there, time slipped away and Davey spoke most freely. As always, his incorrigible cat, Squish, had tagged along. She napped on a nearby V-shaped limb.

"Davey." My voice was barely a murmur.

He didn't budge, a look of concentration on his freckled nine-year-old face.

I swung my feet impatiently, breathing in the damp air. It had been a just-us kind of summer, our schedule set only by the sun. As long as we were home by supper, Mom and Dad let us explore far and wide. It helped that Dad had grown up on Pelican Island himself and knew the way that the streams of the Carolina salt marsh could call out to a kid, begging to be discovered.

Mom was generally supportive of adventure as well—she was the one who had given me a rowboat two years ago, for my tenth birthday. She was a high school biology teacher, so her preference was for adventures with an educational angle. When we were younger, Davey and I helped collect samples for her research projects. But that summer, I had my own secret mission: to get Davey talking again.

My brother had always been quiet, but he'd changed over the last year. With each passing day, his words faded, like something left out in the sun too long. There were times Davey refused to talk to anyone at all.

But that summer, I realized that our special place had its own magic. Out at The Thumb, we sat for hours up in the tree—reading, talking, and listening to the wind. Life was softer there, the edges gently blurred. When I looked out on the horizon, it was impossible to tell the exact place where the sea became sky.

"Davey," I repeated, more firmly this time. "Come on."

I could tell by the way his eyebrow twitched that he

had heard me. He scratched idly at a mosquito bite behind his ear, but his eyes never left the page.

Davey was the type of person who gobbled up words. As a writer myself, I considered him the perfect reader. But writers have jealous hearts, and it burned me to see him devouring words written by another.

Quickly, I plucked a twig and launched it in his direction. It grazed his nose and fell onto the page in front of him.

He brushed it aside without looking up. "Yes, Bex?"

When Davey was a toddler, he couldn't make the sounds for Rebecca. He shortened my name to Bex, and that's what everyone on our island has called me ever since.

"I want to read you something," I said.

Davey squinted, rubbing his nose thoughtfully. He understood how much I'd struggled with my stories. Up until recently, writing had been as natural to me as breathing. But lately, I'd been stuck—instead of filling pages, I was wearing out erasers.

He used his finger to mark his place and then peered at me. "Go on."

Once I had his attention, my mouth turned into a desert. I swallowed hard. I only had a couple of sentences, but maybe they were the start of something good. Something real.

"The sunshine was a bully. The ground dry and parched."

I let the words hang in the air. I checked for his reaction but couldn't read his expression.

"Well?" I asked.

Davey blinked. If he was surprised that I didn't have more written down, he had the decency to hide it.

"The sunshine was a bully—I like that." Davey rolled the words around in his mouth like he was tasting them. "But why say *dry* and *parched* when they mean the same thing?"

The words, which had seemed so glorious a moment ago, felt clunky and wrong. I groaned. "I'll never get it right."

I flipped my pencil over and scrubbed at the page. I'd erased so many times that the paper had worn thin in spots.

Davey leaned forward, eyes wide and earnest. "Listen, Bex. What's that thing you always say about writers?"

I scowled, flicking away eraser crumbs.

"They can't ever lie," I muttered.

Davey nodded. "Writers must tell the truth thoroughly, constantly, and recklessly. Do that and the words will come."

I held up the page, smudged gray from the erasing. "Not likely."

"I know you can do it," Davey said. "Who was the only one brave enough to tell Principal Trout when she had a long piece of toilet paper stuck to her shoe?"

I shrugged. "Me."

Davey smiled in that very specific way he had, where

the left side of his mouth lifted up first and then the right side curled, like it was afraid to be left behind.

He scratched behind his ear again, thinking. "And who was the only one who let Aunt Louise know she'd made her famous blueberry pie with salt instead of sugar?"

My tongue puckered at the memory. "Also me."

He grinned. "See what I mean? You're the best truth-teller I know."

His words loosened the knot that had been forming in my chest all afternoon. "Thanks, Davey."

"Anytime, Bex." He returned to his book.

A breeze rustled the leaves and I settled back against my branch, gazing at a patch of sky.

As far as telling the truth goes, this is a big one: in life, we all need someone to remind us of who we really are. I was lucky enough to have that person as my brother. He always managed to see the best parts of me, even when I couldn't.

CHAPTER 3

The live oak tree grew according to its own logic. More outward than upward, its branches swooped low before spiraling into crisscrossed webs around us, the perfect framing for a view of water or sky.

Davey rummaged in his red backpack, which held a rotation of items, such as favorite rocks or leaves, a beat-up water bottle, and, once, an unusually placid and forgiving frog. But no matter what Davey collected, there were two items that stayed the same: a copy of whatever book he was currently reading and a plastic jar full to the top with yellow M&M's.

Why that color in particular? Davey was convinced they tasted best and wouldn't touch the other ones. It never made much sense to me—because color isn't a flavor. But every time Mom filled the glass bowl on her desk, Davey picked out all the yellows.

He unscrewed the lid and carefully took out two. He tossed one to me, and I caught it, popping it into my mouth. The sweetness spread across my tongue just as sure as sunshine. During times like these, I had to admit that Davey was onto something.

I aimed at his book with my chin. "What are you reading, anyway?"

Davey raised it so I could see the tattered cover, which any kid would recognize immediately. It was a *crying* book—my least favorite. It was the kind where one of the characters dies at the end, which is the worst kind of crying book there is.

I shook my head. "Again? What's the point of getting to know a character only to have them killed off?"

Over the years, my parents and teachers have labeled me as "contentious," which means that I was born to argue. My brother was naturally easygoing—but because he knew how much I loved a good squabble, he'd never dream of letting me win without a fight. This was one of the things I loved best about him.

Davey's skinny shoulders heaved in a dramatic sigh. "You wouldn't understand, Bex."

"Try me," I said, blowing at the strands of hair plastered to my forehead—the irregular line of bangs I'd trimmed last week. Meanwhile, Davey scratched his forehead like he was thinking deep. He didn't seem anywhere near as hot and miserable as I was. His dark hair was freshly combed. Sprays of freckles stood out against his fair skin.

"I like books that make me feel things," Davey said finally. "I think that's the entire point of a book."

I waved my arms in wide circles. "But why in the world would anyone ever choose sadness when there are so many other things to be? I'd rather feel happy because someone is winning a gazillion dollars. Or scared because someone is fighting a monster. Or *curious* because of a puzzle or a surprising twist."

"The *whole* book isn't sad," Davey said stubbornly. "It's mostly happy, except the part at the end."

"But looking back at it, it messes up the whole story," I told him. "How can you read the whole thing again knowing something bad is about to happen?"

Davey loosened the jar lid. He lobbed another candy in my direction before placing one in his mouth.

"If a book is sad and stays that way, then it *would* be depressing," Davey said slowly. "But this book starts happy, gets sad, and then at the end, it's happy and sad mixed up together. That's what makes it special, that it has both."

"But it'll break your heart." This time, *my* voice sounded stubborn.

"Worth it," Davey said, opening his book again.

I turned over the M&M in my mouth, considering his words. My brother was a bit of a genius—not the boring kind who always knew the answer. The good kind, who asked questions that my own brain could never think up. The kind who helped me see the world differently. Sometimes I thought that was why he'd always been on the quiet side—it was as if he needed to conserve energy to power the enormous gears in his brain.

I shifted on the branch, the deep furrows of the tree pressing their pattern against my back. Even on a hot day, the marsh was full of life. Thick thatches of smooth cordgrass rose up like islands among the deep-blue streams. Fiddler crabs scuttled along the shore's sandy edges. Terrapins clambered onto logs, soaking up sunbeams for the energy they'd need when hunting their supper. Even the mussels had their own quiet purpose, holding their shells wide enough to filter food particles into their tiny mouths.

Sunshine dappled the water and made me squint. I searched for the clownish pair of otters we'd spotted earlier. Davey had wasted no time in naming them Fritz and Opal, after the brother and sister from the *Binky Bunnies* cartoon we'd loved when we were small. We decided that Fritz and Opal must be young because they were so playful, splashing and rolling as much as they searched for food. And when they were successful with the crawdad or turtle or shrimp they pursued, their chittering celebration echoed throughout the marsh.

Then, from the corner of my eye, I noticed something strange.

I studied it for a moment, puzzled. Too firm for an animal. Too unyielding for a plant.

My heart pounded. I scrunched my eyes up tight and counted slowly to thirty. I didn't want to alert Davey and get his hopes up only to realize that I'd been taken in by a shadow or floating stick.

But when I looked again, it was still there. One, two, three, four, *five* shapes poked above the surface of the water. They were completely still.

I scooted way out to the end of my branch. Then I hooked my legs and flipped upside down to get a better look. That was when I saw it.

CHAPTER 4

If you read the first page, I told you exactly what to expect: a hand. That's the truth.

But even when the same word is used, people imagine different things. For example—if I said "hand," Mom would automatically think about muscles and bones and veins and tendons and all the biology stuff. Dad loves poetry, so he would probably consider how a hand can be soft like flower petals or something goofy like that.

Some people might picture a disgusting chopped-off object floating in the water, even though I already told you I don't like books about dead things.

It wasn't that kind of hand at all. It was made of metal. It was part of a statue.

The thing about writing is this: if you go a few lines

and realize the story isn't right, you can take the words back. It's easy to erase—to zip them back just as I would with the line on a fishing reel.

It's not always that way. Sometimes things can't go back to exactly how they were before—like if you say unkind words to someone. Our neighbor Mrs. Ochoa would say that's like toothpaste. Once it comes out of the tube, you can't replace it.

That's why writing is so great. If you don't like something, you can try again—squeezing and shaping the words like modeling clay until they make sense. You can back up and start again until you're happy.

CHAPTER 5

"Davey," I said. "You have to see this."

Davey glanced in my direction. Then he looked back sharply. When he realized that I was hanging from my knees, he slammed his book shut and sat up straight.

"Bex! What are you doing? You'll break your neck!" His voice was stern, which only made me giggle.

I swung back and forth, which made the branch shake. "Just *try*, Davey—it's fun!"

"Absolutely not!" he answered. "You're going to make this whole tree fall over."

I opened my mouth, about to tease him for being afraid. But when I noticed how pale he'd turned under his freckles, I hoisted myself back onto the branch. "Sorry. Come see, okay? There's something in the water."

Davey nodded and I was forgiven. He inched over onto my branch. We lay flat on our bellies and craned our necks to the side.

I pointed. "Over there."

Davey's eyebrows wrinkled in a frown. "What is it?"

"I have no idea. But I'm going to find out."

Before Davey could stop me, I'd already jumped onto the next bough, sidestepped Squish (who twitched her tail judgmentally), and slid down the tree.

I kicked off my sneakers and waded into the marsh, treading carefully to avoid the wrack that lined the shore. Wrack was dried-out cordgrass, which turned pale after it died. It washed in and out with the tide, floating on top of the water. For some reason, it always seemed to collect around The Thumb. At some point, Davey had taken to calling this area the River Sticks, which I think was a reference to something in mythology. Davey had a lot of genius jokes like that.

By the time Davey made his cautious climb down from the tree, I was in past my ankles.

"Watch out for snakes!" he called. "Don't walk on any oyster shells!"

Not for the first time, I wondered how two people so different could have been born to the same parents. But when I glanced back and noticed him chewing his bottom lip and wiggling his nervous feet, my heart softened up real fast. I didn't have to see Davey to know what he would think or say or do—when I closed my eyes, I could feel it in my heart. That's how it was with Davey and me.

"I promise it's fine," I yell back. "It's only the River Sticks, nothing to be afraid of!"

Davey plopped down, cross-legged. One hand clutched his red backpack to his chest. The other petted Squish, who must have scrambled down behind him.

As the water deepened, sticky mud sucked at my feet. Normally, the fish would dart away, but they seemed listless. There was nothing cool or refreshing about this water.

Then something skimmed across my hand. I drew back in time to see a blue crab swimming away. At the nearby shore, an audience of small fiddler crabs stood watching.

"There sure are a lot of crabs here," I said over my shoulder. "Blues and fiddlers."

"Please be careful, Bex," Davey cried. "One wrong step and that mud will swallow you up!"

Marsh mud—called pluff mud—could be dangerous. But I knew how to walk carefully and which spots to avoid.

"Make sure you shuffle your feet," Davey added.

I ignored him, holding my breath as I approached. Part of me wondered if the hand had been a trick of the light—or if the mysterious object would sink and I'd never know what it was. But as I moved closer, the thing in front of me only looked more real.

I reached out and touched metal, smooth and solid.

"They're fingers, Davey!" I shouted, my voice cracking with glee. "It's a hand!"

Under the surface were a wrist and the beginnings of an arm. The object was bigger than I was—maybe even bigger than Dad. It was made of metal with a greenish cast and it glistened in the water.

"I think it's a statue," I yelled. "But it's too murky to see much."

"Be careful!" Davey fussed.

The ground sloped downward. "The water gets deeper here! I'm going to go under."

He gasped. "Don't you dare, Bex! We aren't supposed to swim without an adult!"

I took a deep breath and ducked my head under the surface. Although I couldn't see clearly, I could feel it. Made of the same material as the hand, strangely cool in the warm water.

I stood up fast. "It *is* a statue! A whole person!"

Davey's jaw dropped open, but I didn't pause for conversation. I stuck my head underwater again. This time, I didn't bother opening my eyes. Instead, I traced the statue with my hands. Under the water, I located a head, a torso, and a pair of legs. I pushed at it to see if it would move—but it didn't budge.

Eventually, I had enough. As I returned to shore, I couldn't stop grinning. Worry radiated off Davey. I don't think he breathed deep until I was back on solid ground.

He didn't speak when I got there but simply handed me a candy. He usually measured them out carefully to make them last. Another M&M immediately after the ones in the tree meant he really *was* upset.

"I didn't mean to scare you," I said. "I'm okay, see?"

Davey pinched his nose. "You stink—and you're covered in slime."

Even though he wouldn't admit he was worried, I knew he was relieved to see me next to him once more. I looked down at my legs. Pluff mud was the stickiest, gooiest substance in the universe. Some people, like Davey, thought its odor was like rotten eggs. To me, the scent was strong but not unpleasant. It was interesting and rich, the smell of all the life that the marsh had ever contained—the result of thousands of years of river and ocean mingling with each passing of the tides.

I rubbed my left foot against my right shin. "It's not so bad."

Davey's eyes twinkled. "If Mom sees you, you are going to be in *so* much trouble."

Without answering, I scooped a handful of mud from my legs and launched it at him. It landed in a splatter, falling short of him by several inches.

He ran back, shrieking and laughing.

I shook my fist, pretending to be mad. "You better watch out or I'll turn you into a slime monster, too!"

He shuddered, grinning. "Better not!"

I wrung out the bottom of my T-shirt, releasing a cascade of water. "Let's go back so I can change clothes."

Davey placed Squish in the boat and then climbed in. I buckled my life jacket before launching us into the water. My mind spun with questions. I didn't know what the statue was or where it came from. But I knew that I had to find out.

CHAPTER 6

On Dad's truck, there was a bumper sticker that said, "You can't buy happiness, but you can buy a boat," and that's how I felt about the *True Blue*. She represented freedom and I loved every inch of her, from the high sides that Davey liked to rest against to the wooden seats to the oars that balanced perfectly in my hands as I pulled us through the water. Boats have their own personalities, and the *True Blue* was thoughtful and sturdy, the perfect friend to Davey and me.

My brother bubbled over with questions. "Who do you think put the statue there? What is it made of? How did it get out there in the marsh?"

It made me smile to see his excitement. Before answering, I rowed a few strokes, flexing the muscles in my back and arms as we traveled through the smooth water. The feeling of happening upon a big mystery was absolutely delicious. I knew exactly how Davey and I would be spending our summer.

"I have no idea. It was solid, too. Heavy."

Davey's eyes squinched in a frown. "We didn't see it yesterday. Do you think someone put it in the water last night?"

I navigated around a patchy island of cordgrass. "It's stuck deep in the mud. I think it's been there a long time—the water level finally lowered enough for us to see it."

Davey's eyes widened. "Bex! What if it's from a pirate ship?"

Something told me that the statue wasn't *that* old, but I didn't want to discourage him. It had been so long since he'd talked like this. "Maybe. There weren't any markings on it."

"I bet it's pirate treasure," Davey said confidently. "We should ask Mom and Dad. They might know something about it."

I hesitated. The discovery was important—*special*. Davey had been so quiet lately. I knew Mom and Dad were worried. I'd become used to their conversations suddenly halting the moment I entered the room, and I was sure they were talking about him.

When we were out at The Thumb, things were different. Davey and I always felt happier and freer when we were there. And the statue was the kind of project he'd get really excited about. Maybe it was a way to help him. We should keep it to ourselves, for a little while anyway. If other people got involved, his spark of curiosity might flicker out.

But I didn't want to say that *directly*.

"Let's see what we can figure out on our own, without telling anyone else."

Davey tilted his head. "But why?"

"Remember two years ago, when you went through your detective novel phase?"

Davey sat up straighter. He took pride in the breadth and depth of his reading interests.

"Of course," he said happily. "I love surprise twists. Every good mystery has one."

I smiled to myself. "In any of those books, did the kids ever tell an adult about what they were doing? Even when the whole investigation could have been cleared up with one simple conversation?"

Davey frowned, prodding a mosquito bite on his knee.

I cleared my throat. "Besides, things change once adults stick their noses in. It will be their project, not ours."

Davey seemed to think that over. "How will we learn about the statue if we can't ask anyone?"

"Obviously, the Internet," I answered.

His eyebrows drew together. "No one ever uses the Internet in books."

I grinned. "*We* can, though, because this is real life."

Davey chewed his lip thoughtfully.

I squinted at the sun reflecting off the water. "We'll tell them after we know a little more. Promise."

He nodded. "All right, Bex. We'll keep it to ourselves—for now."

With his words, he leaned back and closed his eyes. He did this sometimes as I rowed, and I didn't mind. He always trusted me to get us where we needed to go. Besides, he needed time to be quiet with his thoughts, so his giant brain could think.

My rowing found a rhythm as the oars cut through the water with a familiar *woosh-plop* sound. As we traveled, I wondered what other secrets the marsh might contain. It was a place of extremes coming together. Sometimes the water was fresh and sometimes it was salty. Sometimes it flooded and sometimes it drained. It was not a river and not an ocean, not one thing or another but somehow both.

"Ptooey," Davey spat, and I realized I'd steered us into a cloud of gnats.

"Sorry." The marsh was home to all manner of bugs. Really, the place belonged to them and the rest of us just visited.

Soon enough, our dock came into view. Davey crouched, ready to leap onto the dock. My brother had practiced this jump enough that he always landed with a knee-wobbling *thunk*.

"Nicely done," I said, tossing the line. When we got close enough, I placed Squish on the dock and she twisted against Davey's legs like they'd been separated for hours. He scooped her up and she gazed at him, blinking. Davey once told me that was how cats said "I love you," and he would know. He's an expert.

Together, we looped the rope around the cleat, wrapping it around, up, and forward until it made an infinity symbol.

We scrambled up the short incline to our house. Slung low to the ground, it had white siding, a brick chimney, and flower boxes under the windows. Most of the house was on the first level, but at some point, a spiral staircase and a second story had been added—one small bedroom for Davey and one for me.

I was reaching for the screen door when Davey yanked at my sleeve. With his other hand, he pointed at the open kitchen window. I could just barely hear the faint strains of the music for Mom's favorite podcast. I froze. Usually, Mom left her kayak out to drain. When I hadn't seen it at the dock, I assumed she was gone. If Davey hadn't stopped me, I would have strolled inside slimy and goo-covered. Mom would ask how it happened and Davey always crumbled under direct questioning.

Before I could whisper "thank you," he turned and sprinted away. I followed, running quickly and quietly. That was the thing about having a brother like Davey. Even without words, we understood each other a lot better than most people do.

CHAPTER 7

With the garden hose, I rinsed off the worst of the muck.

Of course I couldn't resist spraying an arc of water toward Davey, who giggled and ducked under the stream. We played like that for a while—him dodging and me chasing him with the water.

"Hey, Bex! Hi!"

It was Millie Ochoa-Chen, waving wildly to us, a basket over one arm. My stomach tightened. There's nothing like a used-to-be friend to take a happy moment and turn it into marsh mud.

"Oh," I said flatly. "Are you visiting again?"

Her grandma, Mrs. Ochoa, lived next door.

Millie squinted at me. "Every summer since I was six, remember?"

I remembered, all right. I used to look forward to those visits. Millie had many talents—besides speaking three languages, she was double-jointed in her thumbs and roasted perfect marshmallows. Her dad was Taiwanese-American and her mom was Mexican-American and Millie attended an immersion school in San Francisco. She was generous with her knowledge and had taught Davey and me how to say "fart," "butt," and "snot" in Mandarin, Spanish, and French. But at the end of last summer, something changed between Millie and me. I knew it would never be the same again.

I watched Davey sidle closer. He didn't want to miss our discussion.

Millie followed my gaze. When she looked back at me, she was frowning faintly. "Why are you randomly getting water everywhere? It's not good for the lawn."

Millie had changed. Last summer, she would have joined in. She might have pulled out the water blasters that Mrs. Ochoa kept in her garage—she always saved the yellow one for Davey. But it seemed that Millie had become too mature for life in general.

"It wasn't *random*," I said. "I'm rinsing off."

Millie rolled her eyes. "*Ooo*okay," she said, stretching the first syllable out long. "You were getting it on the grass, though. My grandma says it's important not to overwater. Plus, didn't you hear that there's a drought?"

I switched off the spigot with a squeak. Davey leaned against the house casually, looking back and forth between us. I could feel his ears straining to listen. Davey was curious by nature and I never told him why Millie and I stopped being friends.

Millie's hair had grown since last summer. She wore it in one long, glossy ponytail and with a clip that matched the pink flowers on her dress. Delicate gold jewelry swung from her ears. It was basically the outfit of a grown-up.

Millie pointed to my hair. "You got bangs."

I shrugged, pushing them to the side. "I did it myself. They're kind of uneven."

"I like it," she said.

I snorted. "My mom didn't."

Millie laughed. "I bet."

I grinned back for a moment—then I remembered that we weren't friends anymore.

Millie touched her earrings, which shone against her warm beige skin. "Bex, is everything okay? How come you never wrote back to my letters?"

Ugh. There was no good way to answer that, especially because I'd shoved them in my desk drawer, unread. It was easier to ignore Millie when she was thousands of miles away. Sometimes my whole life needed a desk drawer where I could stuff all the complicated and difficult things.

I decided to change the subject. "What do you have there?"

Millie's eyes widened, like she'd forgotten the basket

on her arm. "Grandma got these in the store. She's collaborating with a jam maker and making all kinds of cool flavors."

She handed it to me. Nestled inside a blue gingham cloth were several jewel-colored jars of jam, including blackberry habanero, cucumber mint, and guava fig. Mrs. Ochoa's store was like a little farmers' market, with lots of locally produced items. These had a label on them that said Gingerbread Island, which was several islands north of here.

"That's nice—thanks." Mrs. Ochoa was always making us an extra batch of soup or a casserole or cookies. It was nice to have a neighbor like that. It wasn't Mrs. Ochoa's fault that I was mad at Millie.

Millie paused. "We could hang out this summer. I'll be around, you know. Unless you're busy."

Davey raised his eyebrows at me. I could tell he was wondering if Millie could help with the statue. Davey always wanted everyone to get along.

I shot him a look and then turned back to Millie. "I am pretty busy doing stuff for my mom. You know how it is."

Millie nodded slowly. "Right, how is she doing?"

Fifteen years ago, Mom came to the island to do research in the marsh. My dad was the reason she stayed. After all this time, she says sometimes she feels like an outsider—as if people are wondering if she'll stay. Islanders can be funny like that. Dad, Davey, and I were born here. But even though Mom has lived here for a long time, sometimes she's still treated as new.

So it burned me a bit that Millie was asking after Mom. Millie wasn't an islander, of course, even though her grandma was. I didn't want Millie to think she could check on Mom like that.

"Great," I said, more sharply than I intended. "Fantastic, actually. She's never been better."

Millie gave me an odd look but then smoothed the front of her dress. "If you end up having time, you know where to find me."

She walked back to Mrs. Ochoa's and went inside. The screen door slammed shut behind her.

Davey waved goodbye, then turned back to me. "Millie's nice. How come we aren't friends with her anymore?"

I returned the hose to its reel, pretending not to hear him.

"Maybe she could help us investigate the statue," Davey added.

I scowled. "We said we weren't going to tell anyone."

Davey shook his head. "We said we wouldn't tell any *adults*."

I groaned. As much as I usually loved it when my brother argued with me, this was not the time or the place for it. I knew what I was doing. Back in the boat, he had been overflowing with questions. I'd heard him talk more than I had in a long time. But as soon as Millie was around, he got quiet again.

"It's *our* adventure, no one else's. Okay?"

He chewed his bottom lip. Finally, he nodded. "Just us. Davey and Bex."

That settled it. I breathed a sigh of relief. We had a plan for the summer, and it was going to fix everything I'd been worried about. The secret of the statue had to be kept to Davey and me.

CHAPTER 8

We rummaged around in the bin on the screened porch looking for old towels, then dried ourselves the best we could.

Davey crossed to the screen door and I followed—but instead of going inside, he stopped short.

I poked him in the side. "Whatcha doing?"

He waved his hand to shush me, so I craned my neck to see.

Mom stood at the counter and stared out the window. Somehow, she looked smaller and more tired than usual. Her brown ponytail was flat, like it was tired, too.

It was obvious to me that she was concerned about Davey. I swallowed hard. Something told me that if Davey knew we were worried, he would feel awkward. That wasn't the way to get someone's words unstuck. I had to explain away our parents' worry, instead of letting on that he was at the center of it.

"Mom is fine," I murmured. "She's working a lot."

Davey hesitated, but I pushed open the screen door anyway.

"Hey, Mom!" I used a little extra volume to pull her out of her thoughts. I dropped the basket on the counter next to her. "This is from Mrs. Ochoa."

Mom stood up straight, startled. "That was kind of her. And I still haven't returned her pie plate from last week." She gestured vaguely at the counter, where a hand-painted ceramic dish sat.

"I'll take it back," I said quickly. Mom didn't need one more thing to worry about.

"You're sweet." Mom kissed me on top of the head. She paused, noticing my damp hair. "And *wet*. Why are you so wet?"

Davey stifled a giggle behind his hand.

I inched backward. "Just messing around with the hose, Mom."

Mom reached out, squeezing my shoulder. Her eyes took in the jagged line of my bangs. She stared at me for so long, I started to wonder if I'd missed some of the marsh goo. But when I looked at her face, the corner of her mouth quirked up. I was glad to have a mom who wasn't against a little adventure.

Adventure. I thought again of the five fingers reaching up from the murky water. My insides were bursting with anticipation. I couldn't wait to start solving that mystery— *our* mystery. Davey's and mine.

"Mom, can I use your laptop?"

I'd barely finished my sentence before Mom was shaking her head. "You need to shower before I can consider answering that question. And hurry—Dad's coming home between shifts and I want us to sit down for supper together."

I winced. The idea of waiting until evening was almost too much to bear. I opened my mouth to argue, but she fixed me with an I-mean-it look. Davey gave me a warning glance. He knew if I pushed it, we might not be able to use the computer at all.

He pointed at the stairs in a way that said, "Race you!"

Before I could answer, his feet were already on the third step. I'm older so I should be quicker, but Davey practically teleported up those stairs. By the time I reached the second floor, he was disappearing into his bedroom. Through the door, I could hear Squish meowing. To me, it always sounded like complaining, but Davey would probably say she was trying to talk him into opening a can of tuna fish for a special before-dinner snack.

I hummed to myself as I picked out fresh clothes and then went to wash up. When I returned to the kitchen, Mom and Davey were already at the table, and Dad was dishing up plates. Davey had changed into fresh clothes, even though he hadn't gotten dirty. He was particular about those kinds of things.

"Hey there, Bex-Bean," Dad said, which was what he always called me.

Dad was a giant of a man, with curly red hair that was slightly thinning on top, a red beard, and a big barrel chest. His naturally light skin had turned rough and ruddy from being on the water so much, with layered freckles dusting his arms and cheeks. Davey got the same freckles but otherwise took after Mom, with the same slight build and long-lashed blue eyes. I got Dad's sturdiness, the same brown eyes that crinkled when we smiled, and the same love of the water and adventure.

Davey read at the table, lingering over a few last pages before the no-books-at-mealtimes rule officially began. His legs were pulled up crisscross, and Squish sprawled across his lap. He gently rubbed behind her silky ears. She was a calico—white with patches of orange and black. They're known for being especially opinionated, and Squish's main opinion was this: Davey was the best human in our household, possibly in the entire world.

The forks and napkins were already out, because that was Davey's job. I began to fill water and milk glasses. Dad carried over the plates and we sat down together.

"Is this the red drum I caught? It's absolutely delicious," Dad said.

Mom nodded. "And the kale from Mrs. Ochoa's market. She sent over some jams, too."

"Kale," I muttered. "Blargh."

Davey giggled. Dad ignored us, swallowing a hearty bite. "Good old Mrs. Ochoa. She's always looking out for us, isn't she?"

He reached over and squeezed Mom's hand.

Davey crossed his eyes at me. Our parents were affectionate like that. They'd been married for ages, and still Dad took the stairs double when he came home from the ferryboat, like he couldn't wait to lift Mom off her feet into a giant bear hug. He liked to say that it was those same hugs that convinced Mom to come live with him on this island forever, so he couldn't let his skills get rusty.

Dad released Mom's hand but continued to look at her. "How was your day? Anything new to report?"

Mom launched into an explanation of the day's research.

Mom had been in grad school when she first came to Pelican Island—she spent a few months here researching bacteria and also met Dad. When the research trip ended, Mom left, too, at first. But then she couldn't forget my dad. So she switched from the idea of being a full-time researcher to the idea of being a high school biology teacher. On every break, though, she went right back to spending as much time in the marsh as she could.

While they talked about the samples, I stared at my plate. My brain was buzzing. There was no way to fake being interested in her stories about water and sand when all I could think about was the statue. "Don't you think so?" Mom asked.

I jumped in my seat. Davey knew I'd been caught day-dreaming. He hid a laugh behind his hand.

Dad's eyes twinkled. "Mom was talking about the crabs."

Mom nodded, glancing around the table. "I haven't seen as many this year. Maybe it's due to the drought."

I shrugged. "I found a bunch today."

Davey's eyes widened and I realized my mistake. Oh no. Why did I say that? The last thing we needed was Mom poking around the statue.

Mom's eyes brightened, leaning forward. "You did? Where?"

I thought quickly. "Mooney Park."

The little playground with tire swings was on the way to town—in the opposite direction of The Thumb.

Mom raised her eyebrows. "In that part that slopes down toward the marsh?"

My stomach clenched. I didn't like misleading her.

"Mmm," I said vaguely.

Davey caught my eye with a sympathetic look. He knew I was serious about telling the truth and that it pained me to do anything different. He nodded slightly as if to say that sometimes it was okay to have a different version of the truth, if it was necessary.

To avoid further discussion, I took a big forkful of food

from my plate. Unfortunately, I'd already finished the fish. Which meant I was chewing a big, rubbery mouthful of kale.

I washed it down with half a glass of milk. "Wow, this kale is really . . . something! It barely even tastes like dirt."

Davey smirked. Genius as he was, he had decided long ago that the brain-fuel benefits of vegetables outweighed the downsides—he always ate them first.

"Listen," Mom said, changing the subject. "It's summer and you know what that means—it's time for our annual clean-out."

Davey and I exchanged glances. Some families had summer vacation spots they went to, but *our* family had weeks on end where we examined each and every toy, book, and piece of clothing in the house before sorting it into Keep or Donate piles. This was a yearly struggle, especially because my brother and I were the type of people to grow attached to things.

"Take a day or two and get it done, or work on it a little at a time over the course of the summer," Mom continued. "But if I don't see progress, I'll jump in and take over."

She reached over and tapped Dad's arm. "This means you, too. I'm talking about that holey T-shirt collection of yours."

Dad laughed and shook his head. "I go way back with those shirts! I've known some of them since high school."

Mom grinned. "Exactly my point."

Dad put down his napkin, sighing. He knew when he was beat. "Thanks for supper. Sorry I have to head back for another shift."

"Summer's the busy season," Mom said. "We understand, right?"

Davey and I nodded. The rest of the year, the ferry stopped running around seven p.m., but in season it went until midnight. It was to encourage the seasonal renters to travel from island to island, visiting the beaches—and spending their money.

Dad got to his feet. He leaned over to give Mom a kiss. Then he put on his ball cap, turning to look at us. "Want to come along? It will be a late night, but I'll provide unlimited funds for the snack bar."

I glanced at Davey, who shrugged. Riding along with Dad was one of our favorite things to do. When we were small, he would take us with him all the time—he'd set up this box for us to nap in, and the rest of the time he'd wear us in this baby-carrier contraption. As we got older, we'd sit next to him, listening to the poems he wrote about the sea. Dad always said water and poetry were his religion, that he drew a kind of calmness and strength from them that other people got from church.

Mom tilted her head in the direction of her desk. "Thanks, but I've got to catch up on recording my data." She stood up and went to the sink, filling the big copper kettle. In one hand, she held the striped box of tea, her favorite for nights when she was working late. To me, the smell of peppermint was forever intertwined with the rhythm of Mom's fingers tapping at the keyboard, broken by the occasional rustling sound of her searching through one of her notebooks.

I shot a look at Davey. If Mom had to work, we wouldn't get any computer time. He raised his eyebrows as if to say that maybe we should go along with Dad. Visiting the ferry had been more fun since Dad decided we were old enough to explore by ourselves. The crew knew us well, and Mary Ellen at the snack bar put extra butter on our popcorn.

But I didn't want to be up late tonight. Low tide came early in the morning.

"Another time, okay, Dad?" I said.

"Of course," he said. He lowered his voice so Mom couldn't hear us from the kitchen. "Please help with the dishes. Mom's been so tired lately—she needs your support."

"All right," I said as Davey nodded.

Dad gave goodbye hugs and scratched Squish behind the ears. We heard him whistling a tune as he walked out to his truck in the driveway. Then the engine roared and he drove away.

While Davey and I washed the dishes, Squish twisted around my legs, demanding attention.

Mom drizzled a thin stream of honey into her mug.

"Do you need anything before I get started? I could whip up some peanut butter popcorn if you like."

I thought of Dad's words. I didn't want her to do anything extra.

"No thanks," I said.

She looked at me carefully. "Are you sure? There's been so much going on this summer—I know you said you wanted to have your own adventures, but I've been missing our time together."

"Positive," I said.

Mom reached over and tucked a piece of hair behind my ear. "I'm getting used to the bangs. They're cute."

I grinned, watching as she carried her mug to the nook off the living room where a desk crowded in alongside the shelves that held her logbooks—fourteen years of research on water levels, temperatures, and biological activity. Within moments she was settled, typing at her laptop—completely absorbed.

Wordlessly, I grabbed a pint of strawberry-buttermilk ice cream, and Davey and I slipped out the door to the back porch. The air smelled like salt and possibilities. We talked about the statue and told ghost stories. Squish even let me rub her behind the ears for a while before jumping into Davey's chair.

We stared at the sky until our eyes were so tired that we could barely tell the stars from the fireflies. And then we crawled into our beds and went to sleep.

CHAPTER 9

The next morning, after bowls of cornflakes, Davey and I went out to the dock.

I crouched to untie the *True Blue*. Squish rubbed against my shins, looking at me questioningly.

"Of course," I said, placing her in the hull of the boat. She immediately claimed her spot beside Davey, her purr a soft rumble.

The oars were cool in my hands but warmed quickly as I rowed. "Do you think the water will be even lower today?"

Davey shrugged and closed his eyes. I could tell by the look on his face that he was thinking deeply and probably wouldn't speak until we'd reached The Thumb.

With my brother, there was always something below the surface. The marsh was like that, too. From a distance, someone might glimpse the brackish water and patches of green cordgrass and think there was nothing more to see. But the marsh was never meant to be a picture postcard. Instead, it was made of small moments that could only be appreciated up close.

A heron waded nearby—in an instant, it speared a fish with its razor-sharp beak, swallowing it whole in a sudden flash of silver. A pair of dragonflies buzzed past, inches from my nose, then vanished into the tall grass. The morning mist hadn't yet burned off, but already the marsh hummed with its own quiet energy.

Even if Davey's eyes were open, we wouldn't see the same things. In a rowboat, the rower always faces backward. From where they sat, Davey and Squish could see where we were going—but I was always looking where we had been.

The clouds from above reflected clear and crisp. If it hadn't been for the fact of gravity and the resistance against my oars, I might have thought we were drifting through the sky.

Unlike Davey, words have always been a comfort to me. Even though stories weren't coming out on paper the way I wanted, I could still make them in my head. If Davey knew, he'd laugh and say I was showing off. But really, I was just trying to make sense of the world around me. Which is maybe what every good writer is trying to do, when it comes down to it.

When we arrived at The Thumb, Davey blinked, smiling in that lopsided way he had. We both hopped out when the water was shallow and then pushed our boat onto the sand, avoiding the sticks that sprouted along the shore.

"The River Sticks," Davey said in a singsong voice as he sidestepped a patch of wrack. He'd been so quiet in the boat, but now his excitement over the statue was electric. His eyes glinted in the sunshine, his hands gesturing wildly as he talked.

I smiled at my brother, soaking up his chatter. But then something over his shoulder caught my eye. On the trunk of the live oak, someone had painted an orange "X." I stared at it, confused.

Davey followed my gaze. When he saw the marking, he let out a low whistle.

The hair on the back of my neck stood up. I glanced around—but as always, there was no one there but us.

"Who would do this?" Davey asked.

I shook my head slowly. "I have no idea. You keep an eye out while I go check on the statue."

Davey scooped up Squish in his arms. "I don't like it. We should go home."

"Not a chance," I answered.

He bit his lower lip. I knew he felt nervous. It *was* unsettling that someone had clearly been in our spot—but there was no way we could leave without exploring the statue.

"It's okay, Davey. Probably some teenagers messing around," I said.

At this, he seemed to relax.

I turned toward the water. I'd planned ahead, wearing a swimsuit under my clothes. I dropped my shirt and shorts in a pile and stepped in.

After I was up to my knees, I turned back to look at Davey. "Come with me?"

He frowned. "I'm the lookout, remember?"

Something in his voice told me that it had nothing to do with keeping watch—that Davey wouldn't have joined me anyway—but I didn't want to push. I waded into the water.

"Be careful!" Davey called from shore.

I waved my hand behind me so he'd know I heard him.

We'd timed our journey well. The water was much lower, and more of the statue's arm and head showed above the waterline.

A pair of blue crabs swam near the surface, but I didn't disturb them. Instead, I tried to memorize the figure. The hair coiled in curls. It was difficult to tell its expression only from the eyes, but I could feel the nose under the water. Underneath that, I traced the line of a barely curving mouth.

"Well?" Davey yelled. "Can you guess how old it is?"

I shook my head. "You should come take a look."

Davey didn't answer. Instead, he put a hand up to his ear. "Bex, listen!"

I froze. As soon as I stopped moving, I *felt* it—the low whirring vibration of a motor.

Davey's eyebrows arched. Boats of any kind were uncommon in the marsh. It sounded like it came from the other side of the peninsula, where the water was rocky and deep.

My first instinct was to hide, and I guess it was Davey's, too. He crossed to the live oak in about two leaps and hurried from one branch to another, Squish tucked under his arm. Quickly, he disappeared into the canopy of leaves.

As the motor roared, I splashed through the goop and headed for shore. I had almost returned to solid ground when I slipped in a treacherous pile of muck and fell right on my rear end. Scrambling to my feet, I made for the climbing tree.

Meanwhile, the engine cut off, and three people got out of the boat. I knew they'd spot me for sure, so I hid behind the trunk. The woman had stripey blond hair in a braid. She wore a flowy polka-dot blouse. One of the men had a green polo shirt and spiky black hair. The other man wore a pink shirt, a plaid tie, and his hair in twists. They all sported construction vests and tall boots.

"There's a kid," the green-shirted man said.

I winced, ducking back—but it was too late. I'd been seen.

The woman took off her sunglasses, squinting in our general direction. "Hello. Hello, little girl!"

I peeked around the trunk. "Hi," I answered. All I had to do was be a regular, ordinary, completely forgettable kid.

The woman moved closer, eyeing me carefully. I must have been a sight, coated in mud up to my knees, my wet hair dripping. She bit her lip. "You aren't out here by yourself, are you?"

My glance flickered upward, toward Davey in the tree. "I'm here with someone."

Her expression was skeptical, but she nodded anyway. She'd probably thought that I was some mud-covered wild-living child, but she seemed to accept the idea that my adult was temporarily out of sight. I'm sure she didn't expect a skinny nine-year-old boy and a grumpy, fluffy cat to be the ones providing supervision.

The back of my neck prickled. No one ever came here besides Davey and me. It was a long haul from the areas where the tourists gathered, with powdery beaches and crystal-blue waters. The marsh, with its coarse sand and salty, pungent smell, was strictly for locals. The Thumb was too scraggly to reach from the island itself, and only small boats could travel through this side of the marsh.

"Jocelyn," the pink-shirted man called, holding up a clipboard.

"Right," she answered. She returned to them. Although I strained to hear bits of their conversation, I didn't understand the meaning of their words: "structure," "thoroughfare," and "revitalization." I looked up at Davey, who seemed as confused as I was. Even Squish twitched her tail, like she knew they were up to no good.

After a long while, Jocelyn approached the tree. She craned her neck, peering around me. "Are you sure you have someone here with you? Do you want a lift somewhere?"

My heart started beating fast. I had to stop Jocelyn from moving closer. The last thing we needed was a bunch of people poking around the statue.

I pointed in the opposite direction. "My dad is over there, fishing behind the cordgrass. I slipped and fell in the mud, so I'm drying off."

This seemed to ease Jocelyn's mind completely. "Do you come here a lot?"

I hesitated. Something told me that it was better if she didn't know that Davey and I came here all the time. What if they had a rule about kids hanging out on their property?

I shook my head quickly. "We live on the far side of the island. My dad thought we should try fishing here, but we haven't been getting any bites."

The lie came out smoothly, which surprised me, but Jocelyn didn't seem to think twice about it. She turned her head, surveying the area. "It's pretty here but so remote—that's got to be boring for a kid your age, right?"

In my head, I came up with a quick list of about a hundred things to do at The Thumb on any given day—for starters, there was climbing the live oak, catching crabs and minnows, wading in the water, skipping stones, looking at clouds. But I could tell she wouldn't understand, so I just nodded.

Jocelyn's eyes shone. "I've got some good news for you. Have you heard about the big project?"

I looked at her, confused. "What project?"

She beamed. "We're developing this area with a road that will eventually connect to a bridge that goes all the way to the mainland. It's really going to help the tourism industry out here." As she spoke, she pointed at different locations. If what she said was true, there would be a road going right on top of the spot where the live oak stood. My cheeks flushed. So *that's* why it had been marked with a spray-painted "X."

"What about the live oak? It's really old," I said, then caught myself. I had to act like someone who didn't come to The Thumb often. "I mean, I *think* it is. I don't really know for sure."

The corners of Jocelyn's mouth turned down. "It has to be removed, which is sad. But we're limited due to the geography in this area."

I squeezed my hands by my sides. "But—"

She held up her hand. "Don't worry—we're committed to maintaining the natural beauty, so we will plant new trees as we develop."

"New trees aren't the same, though," I said quickly. "A live oak is like its own ecosystem—it provides shade and a habitat for a whole bunch of animals."

Jocelyn looked at me carefully, like I'd surprised her. I wanted to smack myself. This was not the way to blend in and be a regular, forgettable kid.

I cleared my throat. "That's what I *heard*, anyway. On the Internet."

She nodded slowly. "You're correct. It isn't the same. Sometimes things have to change, even when it's hard."

I thought of a million arguments to what she said, but I just looked at the ground.

Jocelyn continued. "But remember, this area isn't going to be boring any longer. I'm sure you'll love having a giant movie theater and bowling alley to visit, right here on Pelican Island."

I shook my head. The whole *point* of The Thumb was that it was untouched—that it belonged to Davey and me. "Does it have to be *here*? Shouldn't it be over on the harbor side instead?"

Jocelyn's forehead wrinkled. "This will be the new hub for the island. Once the bridge is built, residents won't have to depend on a ferry schedule."

Dad's face popped into my mind. Did this mean he might lose his job?

I crossed my arms tight against my chest. "People *like* ferryboats."

Jocelyn didn't seem to listen. She arranged her braid, tucking in a few loose ends. "Well, it was nice to chat with you. Enjoy this little spot while you can—it will be a bustling construction zone soon enough. But be patient! Think about all the fun you'll have here someday."

My heart felt like a glob of marsh goo. Jocelyn strode to where the men were waiting in the boat. She hopped in. After grabbing a seat, she turned in my direction to wave. I watched as the boat sped away.

Above me, a breeze rustled the leaves, and Davey let out a deep sigh. My shoulders slumped. A bridge would be terrible for Pelican Island. It would hurt the ferryboats. The statue would be discovered or possibly destroyed. The Thumb would change forever. If our special place got taken away, where would Davey and I go?

"Will they really build a bridge here?" Davey's voice was shaky.

I gritted my teeth. "They'll have to get through me first."

PART TWO

315 days without rain

CHAPTER 10

Even simple foods taste better when they're prepared by someone else. My best example of this was Davey sandwiches.

Davey sandwiches should be impossible to ruin: two slices of toasted oatmeal bread spread with almond butter, a drizzle of raspberry jam, a sliced half of a banana, and, finally, sprinkled with a crunchy layer of crushed potato chips.

In Davey's hands, this was more than a sandwich: it was magic.

In my hands, something always went wrong. The toast: burned. The bananas: thick. The jam was too gloppy, the almond butter too stiff. Of course, I never messed up the potato chips. (It's impossible to mess up potato chips.)

But I wasn't thinking of this when I got home that day.

Maybe it was because I was distracted worrying about the bridge. I should have known they wouldn't be the same without his special touch.

"Sorry," I said when he came into the kitchen. "They aren't as good as yours."

Davey helped himself to a bite. He chewed for a long while and finally swallowed. "Not bad."

I sighed, pushing aside my plate and the half banana on the table, which was already browning around the edges. From Davey's backpack, I retrieved my black composition book. I flipped past the heavily erased first page. We needed a fresh start.

I tapped my pencil against the table. "Which should we investigate first—the statue or what's going on with the bridge? Should we search on Mom's laptop?"

Davey didn't answer. "Come on," I wanted to say. "I can't do this on my own."

But instead, I took a deep breath. My job was to believe in my brother. If I listened long enough, Davey would help me figure out what to do.

I held out a leftover potato chip for Squish. She darted her pink tongue again and again, licking away the salt. When she finished, she dashed away.

"You didn't get permission," Davey reminded me.

Mom usually wanted us to ask before using the computer. If she found out, we might get grounded, which would be the worst punishment possible.

"I guess we could use the ones at the library," I said.

Davey shook his head. "Let's figure out the bridge first. If construction begins, the statue will be discovered or destroyed."

"Town hall." I said the words aloud as I wrote them on the page. "We need to know when the project will start, who's doing it, and what we can do to make it stop."

We loaded our plates in the dishwasher and went outside together. At the end of the driveway, Davey paused.

There were two main routes. To the left was Sea Salt Boulevard, the main thoroughfare on Pelican Island. The walk was shorter but crowded and noisy.

To the right was the longcut—it was a *long*cut instead of a shortcut because it took slightly more time than going on the main road, but it was infinitely more enjoyable. The journey consisted of a series of tiny paths that wound through neighborhoods . . . past Mooney Park with its tire swings and water views, through the backyards of cotton-candy-colored houses with wide front porches, pretty gardens, and flowering crepe myrtle trees. It also smelled of honey-suckle, freshly cut grass, and homegrown roses, which beat Sea Salt Boulevard's asphalt and car exhaust any day of the week.

"Definitely the longcut," I said. "We'll stop at the park on the way back, if it's not too hot."

Davey grinned. He loved to swing. "Should we go see Dad on the ferryboat?"

I shook my head. There would be time for visiting Dad another day. We had other things to do.

As we walked, Davey made a game of kicking a pebble. He booted it farther and farther down the lane, until eventually it landed in a scrubby patch of grass and he couldn't find it anymore.

"Ugh," he said. But after a while, he found another one and began again. I wasn't interested—in my opinion, it was too hot to do anything other than what was strictly necessary.

We took an alley between two brick houses and came out a block from town hall. That name made the building sound grander than it was. One half was a dedicated visitors' center, with leaflets about attractions on the island, fishing boats available for charter, and schedules for the ferryboat. The other half was boring offices.

Davey and I pulled open the big double doors. Sitting at the front desk was Mr. Harris, a former ferry master who still picked up shifts when someone went on vacation. He had deep brown skin, a fringe of white hair, and a round belly. Davey and I had known him since we were little and we always looked forward to the picnic he hosted for the boat workers each spring. After retiring, he worked in the visitors' center, competed in chess tournaments, and knitted ten hats each week for newborns at the hospital in Port Rogers. Mr. Harris knew even more about Pelican Island than I did.

When he saw us, he waved.

"Hey there," he drawled in his low rumble. "Hot

enough for you? What do you think we have to do around here to get a little rain?"

"Hi, Mr. Harris," I answered. "What are you making?"

He held up his knitting needles, orange yarn dangling. "A pumpkin beanie. I know it's still summer, but I'm planning ahead for fall babies."

As we admired the tiny cap, Mr. Harris explained that he would eventually attach a stem and curling leaves to the top. After a while, he put down the needles and looked at us carefully over the top of his glasses.

"Now, I know you're not here to take a walking tour of downtown," Mr. Harris said. "You know everything about this island. In fact, you could probably give that tour yourself! What can I help you with?"

"Have you heard anything about the bridge at The Thumb?" I asked.

Mr. Harris let out a low whistle. "Oh yes, that's been the talk of the island for a while. Don't y'all read the paper?"

Davey and I shifted uncomfortably. I hadn't read our island's weekly paper, the *Pelican Call*, for a very long time. My whole life, I'd imagined writing for it someday—I even had the goal of seeing my name in a byline before I finished middle school. But my writer's block made it feel like the newspaper was laughing at me every time I saw it. It was easier to leave it on the kitchen table, unopened.

"Not really," I said.

Mr. Harris grinned. "No wonder you hadn't heard of

it." He swiveled in his chair to reach a deep drawer and then began to rummage inside. "I think I have it here . . . yes!"

He removed the pink rubber band from a roll of paper and then smoothed it on the desk. It showed a sketch of what the completed bridge would look like.

"Here, you see? This is part of a seven-step program for the county," Mr. Harris explained, rotating the paper so we had a better view. Davey and I leaned over the desk, studying the drawing. Even without looking at Davey's face, I knew we both wore matching frowns.

The sketch depicted a high, arching bridge that connected the mainland to Pelican Island. It included long lines of cars traveling on the bridge. From the looks of the plan, The Thumb would be blocked off entirely. I thought of what Jocelyn had said about the limitations of the space. It seemed they had ignored the natural geography and plopped their bridge right where they wanted it.

Mr. Harris tapped the paper, indicating the far sides of the island. "There'll be lots of growth here, and Pelican Island will be the hub. Real-estate prices will skyrocket."

I studied the paper, noticing the skinny trees that lined either side of the road. Our live oak was nowhere to be seen. Davey sighed.

"But I don't *want* our island to be a hub!"

Mr. Harris chuckled. "I don't know that we have much to do with it at this point. Our quiet little Pelican Island is going to be bustling, that's for sure."

"What about the ferryboats? I heard there might be some changes with that," I said.

Mr. Harris hesitated. "They won't go away anytime soon, but I don't know what will happen long-term. People have a hard time waiting on a schedule when they know they can just drive themselves and get there faster."

I scowled. "What about Dad's job?"

Mr. Harris looked at me gently. "If there's one thing life has taught me, it's that change comes whether we like it or not. But your family will be okay. You will be okay, too."

Mr. Harris's voice sounded dry. He blew his nose into a handkerchief. "Allergies," he explained, sipping from the glass of water on his desk. Then he rerolled the paper, looping the rubber band tightly.

"When is it going to be built?"

Mr. Harris opened the drawer and tucked away the map. "Not until later in the year. That spot is tricky due to the water levels."

Davey stepped square on my foot. When I looked at him, he mouthed the word "pirates."

I stood up straighter. "Oh, one more thing, Mr. Harris?"

Mr. Harris grinned. "Go on."

"Do you know anything about pirate ships? Maybe ones that might have had statues on them?"

He rubbed his chin thoughtfully. "I'm not sure about statues, necessarily, but pirates ran their ships up and down the coast. I'm sure you know about that from history class."

"In the marsh?" Davey whispered in my ear.

"What about back in the salt marsh?" I asked. "Near The Thumb, specifically."

Mr. Harris frowned. "The area around The Thumb is pretty rocky. It would be tricky for a large vessel to make its way over there."

Davey jabbed me in the ribs. I could tell he didn't want to give up on the idea of pirates so easily.

"Maybe the water was deeper hundreds of years ago," I suggested.

"Could be." Mr. Harris's voice sounded skeptical.

A family of tourists burst into the visitors' center then, with lots of questions for Mr. Harris about the best places to find sea glass and shark teeth.

Davey and I waved goodbye to Mr. Harris and backed away until we were outside where we had started.

Out on the sidewalk, Davey and I looked at each other. This was going to be harder than I'd thought. We knew we had to do something. But what?

CHAPTER 11

Davey and I walked home, shoulders slumped. Our fun summer mystery had taken an unhappy turn. Neither of us wanted to think about what life on the island would be like without The Thumb.

When we got home, Davey held up his book.

"I'm going to go read outside," he said.

"Don't forget your tissues," I said.

He blinked. "Tissues?"

"For the sad ending."

I made a little *boo-hoo* noise and wiped away imaginary tears.

"Ha ha," Davey said flatly. He went out the screen door and made a beeline for the big magnolia tree in the backyard. He sprawled out on the grass—within moments, he was completely absorbed in the story.

I pushed my hair out of my eyes. The heat had made me sweat and my bangs were clinging to my forehead. I went upstairs, intending to grab a hair tie from my dresser drawer. But as I passed by Davey's room, something made me look inside. Mom was stretched out on Davey's bed, fast asleep. His patchwork quilt was perfectly pulled up and Squish was curled in a ball by her feet.

I frowned. Mom didn't usually nap during the day, but she'd seemed a little off lately. I reached out and shook her leg.

"Mom," I said. "What are you doing here?"

Mom startled. She rubbed her eyes for a moment before moving into a sitting position. "I was putting away a few things and felt tired. I must have dozed off."

I swiveled my head to take in the room. On the floor sat a cardboard box that was half-full of picture books, a science-fair medal, and a few unpaired socks.

I stopped short. I knew Mom liked things tidy, but it wasn't right to empty someone's room like that when he wasn't even here to ask.

I whirled to look at her. "You can't get rid of Davey's things without asking!"

She blinked several times before answering. "I wanted to get started on our summer clean-out. I didn't think these things were important."

I crossed my arms tightly. "Well, they *are*. He wouldn't want you to get rid of his stuff."

"Okay," she said softly. "It was just a thought. Come here."

She opened her arms wide and I climbed into Davey's bed next to her. With her cool fingers, she traced a slow, swooping figure-eight pattern on my forehead, like she always did when we were sick or upset. I closed my eyes. After a few moments, my breath steadied and my heartbeat calmed.

We sat that way for a while. Then Mom cleared her throat. "Are you hungry? We could rustle up some bowls of macaroni and cheese."

My *favorite*—Davey's too. My eyes popped open. "Really? Dad *hates* macaroni and cheese."

"Correct. That is his single greatest flaw as a human being." Mom grinned. "But he works the late shift tonight, so we can get cheesy. Cheesy, easy."

"*Mom*," I say. "Come on."

She bopped my nose gently. "Pleasey? Lemon squeezy?"

Mom could be goofy sometimes, but she was trying. Parents didn't understand that certain things were important. There was no such thing as outgrowing picture books. Science-fair medals were hard won. Even the unpaired socks had a place—because what if their partners turned up someday only to find that the other had been thrown aside? This is the heartbreak of tidying up.

I pointed at Squish. "No-fleas-y."

Offended, Squish twitched her whiskers and leaped off the bed.

We got to our feet. Mom smoothed out the covers and gave a little nod. She slipped out of the room and went downstairs. I put everything back where it belonged.

————————————

When I went downstairs, Mom was adding the cheese sauce to the noodles. The main secret of making macaroni and cheese from a box is to stir up the sauce separately from the noodles. She heaped our bowls high and handed me a spoon. Davey preferred a fork. He liked to slide an individual piece on each tine and eat them off one by one.

When I finished, I looked at Mom. "Can I ask you one of those questions—you know, the kind where it's about an imaginary situation?"

Mom set down her water glass. "A hypothetical question? Absolutely."

"Let's say there was something you wanted to research—"

Her eyes brightened. "Like a plant or an animal?"

Mom was always hoping that Davey and I would suddenly fall in love with science the way she had.

My mind spun, trying to come up with the right word.

"More like . . . an *artifact*. Let's say you found a piece of, oh, I don't know, art or pottery or whatever—and you didn't know anything about it. What would you do to find out more?"

"In this case, the researcher would try to answer two main questions—*when* and *who*," Mom said.

Davey and I glanced at each other in confusion.

"What do you mean?" I asked.

Mom tightened her ponytail, like she always did when she was thinking hard. "I'd probably try to match it with similar art that was done around the same time period. Of course, knowing the region would help a lot. If I had the right tools, I could analyze the material and when it was made."

Davey kicked me in the shin.

"No—no tools," I said, shooting Davey a dirty look.

Mom was lost in thought. "Another idea would be checking for an identifying mark. Artists used to make symbols or write a line of text somewhere."

I raised my eyebrows at Davey. I hadn't noticed anything like that, but maybe it was hidden underneath the waterline.

Mom tapped her fingertips together. "Now that I think about it, finding a mark would be best. Because if the mark tied the object to a specific person, you would then know approximately when that object was made. It would be like answering two questions in one."

Davey's eyes were so big, I was sure that he was going to give away the statue—or at least, somehow let Mom know that my question was not totally hypothetical.

"Do you think I could use your laptop? To learn more," I said.

The corner of Mom's mouth quirked up. "Of course. Let me know if I can help."

Just as I figured, she was happy to allow computer time when it was for something educational. Davey and I rushed through the dishes and then raced to Mom's desk, squeezing onto the same chair.

But once my fingers were hovering above the keys, I wasn't sure what to type. Underwater statue? Mysterious statue? I settled on: *mysterious underwater statue*.

When the results loaded, my eyebrows shot up high. "Twelve million results!"

I clicked on the first link, which listed the top ten most fascinating underwater statues. As I scrolled, I skimmed the text. An underwater park in Mexico with five hundred sculptures. An eighteen-foot-tall statue in the Bahamas.

"Why would anyone do this?" I muttered.

Davey peered at the screen, pointing at a marble statue.

I paused to read the caption. "Baiae, an ancient Roman town that was a popular resort, sank five hundred years ago due to volcanic activity." I rolled my eyes. "There aren't any volcanoes around here! And our statue wasn't stone; it was metal."

We sat together in Mom's chair, scrutinizing videos and articles. Aside from the ancient Romans, most of the underwater artwork had been placed intentionally. Some were even designed to help marine life, so corals and sponges had safe places to grow. Maybe our statue was placed on purpose, too. But why would someone put a statue in the salt marsh and not tell anyone about it?

At bedtime, my eyes felt like sandpaper. We powered off the computer and went upstairs.

In the hallway, I turned and looked at Davey.

"As soon as it's light out tomorrow, we're going to go out to The Thumb. And we're going to find that mark."

CHAPTER 12

The next day, Davey and I set out over the marsh. As usual, he had his red backpack. He must have been in a good mood because he gave me a yellow M&M right when I got into the boat. I kept it on my tongue to savor it, knowing it might be a while before I saw another.

That day, the wind pushed against us. I had to work extra hard to row. Squish, who was usually a good traveler, ducked underneath Davey's seat. Eventually we made it to The Thumb, and I pushed the boat onto the shore. This time, I'd brought supplies. If the statue had a maker's mark, I was going to find it.

I looped a waterproof flashlight around my wrist and slid on goggles before wading into the water. As I got closer, I could tell that the water level had lowered.

"Be careful, Bex!" Davey shouted.

I looked back and flashed a thumbs-up. Then I turned to the statue. If only I knew what to look for. I circled, waiting for something unusual to catch my eye.

"I don't see anything!" I yelled at Davey.

"It's probably below the waterline," Davey said, as if it were obvious.

I switched on the flashlight, which made a thin but steady beam through the murky water. The statue wore a knee-length dress, with a pendant around its neck. From the ankles down, the statue was lodged in the muck.

I waded back to Davey on the shore. "What if the mark is on the feet, covered in mud?"

Davey's forehead scrunched in concentration. He unzipped the backpack and rummaged inside. He removed my black composition book and flipped it open, past the page I'd made notes on yesterday. Nearby, Squish stalked in the tall grass—she'd probably located an insect of some kind. Squish liked bugs.

Davey handed me a pencil. "Draw it."

That was a good idea. I needed to back up and start again. Then I'd see if I had missed something. I sat next to him and started to draw.

First, I sketched the part above the waterline. Then I outlined what I remembered of the statue's torso. There was another arm, of course, but what position was it in? I closed my eyes and pictured it: the right arm was bent at the elbow, hand on its hip.

Davey watched over my shoulder. "It's wearing a

dress, right? How could you tell it wasn't a robe or something?"

I thought hard, tapping the pen against my chin. "The top part goes in a V shape, like this. Then it gathers at the waist and flares out."

Together, we studied the picture. It was a start, but it needed more. My lines on the page didn't have the specific details. My drawing didn't capture the way the statue made me feel.

I stood up. "Okay, I'm going to try again."

This time, when I waded back out, I went slowly. I examined the head of the statue. A patch of corrosion covered the side of the neck. I reached out to touch the rough surface, unsure why rust had occurred there but not anyplace else.

Then I realized what I'd missed. On the paper, I'd drawn the dress as smooth, but the gray-green metal had been shaped to somehow look like pleats at the shoulder. I ran my hand over the folds and felt the slippery algae that had collected there.

Then I shone my beam lower. Circles were etched onto the bodice of the dress. The algae hadn't appeared randomly. It had grown where the artist had forged the grooves. Intentionally.

I shivered in excitement. "Davey! The dress is patterned."

Davey hopped from foot to foot, like he couldn't stand not knowing. "Come back here and draw it!"

When I returned to shore, he had the composition book waiting. I pushed aside my goggles and added the new details I'd noticed. Davey crowded me for a better look.

"This time, I noticed the algae was in the ridges and grooves," I said. "It seems like it was done on purpose."

Davey looked skeptical. "Mom mentioned distinct marks, not a bunch of circles."

I scowled at the paper. He had a point.

Davey patted my arm. "Don't be mad. We should keep looking, that's all."

I pulled away. "*We?* Maybe *you* should keep looking! If you're such an expert, how come I'm the only one who keeps getting slimy?"

Davey's eyes looked as blue as the sea and just as watery. My stomach dropped. Sometimes we argued, but that was due to my contentious personality. I never wanted to make him sad.

I reached out to give him a sideways hug. He leaned against me.

"Aw, Davey. I'm mad because I want to figure out this puzzle," I said.

He sighed. "I'm frustrated, too. But we'll figure it out eventually. I know it."

I squeezed him. "If the bridge is built here, the statue will be destroyed. I can't stand that idea."

"I'm sorry that I'm not doing my share of going in the water. I would go in there, but you know how I feel about the River Sticks." He shuddered.

"I don't really mind," I told him. "I'm sorry I snapped."

As if he wanted to show me that I was forgiven, he held out a yellow M&M.

I grinned and popped the candy in my mouth. As important as the statue was, Davey was even more important. Davey was essential.

The next time I returned to the statue, I examined the statue's shins and knees. No marks. My heart thudded. Maybe the artist liked being anonymous.

I rose back up to the surface.

"Nothing down here, only legs," I said.

"Keep looking—if there's a mark, you'll find it!" Davey said cheerfully.

I surveyed the entire dress, following the pattern of interconnected circles. Clearly, whoever made the statue had been talented. The circle pattern followed the dress's pleats and folds perfectly.

Frowning, I aimed the beam at the statue's waist. Another circle, large and thick—on the very center of the dress.

It was a *belt*. The circle represented a clasp, which also had etched lines.

I punched at the water, which didn't make me feel better. More lines—that's the last thing I needed. That wasn't a clue—just another place for algae to collect. And what's worse, the lines weren't symmetrical. The artist must have gotten lazy.

I popped up above the water and breathed in deep.

From the top of my head to the tips of my toes, I was coated with mud and slime. I swished my hands in the water, but clumped algae stubbornly clung to my fingers.

This trip had been a waste. We didn't know a single thing more about this statue, and it seemed like we never would.

"I give up," I whispered, backing away slowly.

The statue looked smug, like it knew it had won. Eyes perfectly formed. Hair coiled with precision. One arm up and one on the hip. Grooves in the dress planned so perfectly that the algae made its own pattern. Whoever made this statue was detail oriented. But, for some reason, the lines on the belt buckle weren't even.

I stopped.

No—it couldn't be. That would be too easy.

But what if it was? I never thought it was possible to run in water, but I did my best—splashing and slipping and clawing my way back to the statue. I plunged my head underwater and shone my light on the buckle. One vertical line crossed by three horizontal lines . . . *Wait.* One of the lines was shorter than the others. That had to be intentional. I traced my fingers over the surface, trying to memorize it with my fingers.

This was it; this was the mark. It had to be.

CHAPTER 13

Davey bounced with excitement.

"I knew you'd find it," he kept saying as I rowed us home. I smiled. It was a good thing to have someone who believed in me, even when I couldn't.

At the garden hose, I cleaned up before going inside for lunch. But it wasn't until I chewed my first toasty bite of almond-butter, banana-slice, raspberry-jam, potato-chip goodness that it hit me.

"Davey," I said slowly. "If that's a mark—"

"It *definitely* is," he interrupted in a singsong voice.

I couldn't help but smile. "Even if it *is*, how will we figure out who made it?"

Davey nodded at the laptop on Mom's desk.

"Good idea." I pulled up a chair, my fingers on the keys. "What terms should I put in?"

"Artist symbol? Maker's mark?" he suggested.

The search results showed a list of definitions. The image search was also uninspiring. Nothing seemed exactly like the mark I thought I'd found. My stomach felt heavy with disappointment.

"There's got to be another way," I said.

Davey bit his thumbnail. "We need to ask someone else. I know you want it to be our mystery, but honestly, Bex, I'd rather have a solved mystery. Wouldn't you?"

I sighed, staring at the screen. This felt like a dead end. "We can crack this, I just know it."

Davey looked skeptical. "Maybe we should forget about the artist and try to stop the developers. If the bridge comes, it's going to smash up the statue anyway."

I shook my head. "If we can prove that a famous artist made the statue, the builders won't make their bridge there. The Thumb will stay just how it is now. That's the most important thing."

His shoulders slumped—he was just as frustrated as I was. We needed a break and I knew exactly what to do.

I jumped up from the chair. "Let's go visit Dad on the ferry."

Davey's face brightened. He said goodbye to Squish, and then we went out the back door. The afternoon sun was bright. Millie sat under a tree in her grandma's yard, reading a book. When she saw us, she raised her head. "Hi!"

"Hey," I said but kept walking.

Davey waved at her and then hustled to catch up with me. "What's going on with you and Millie?"

I shoved my hands in my pockets and pretended not to hear him.

"Come on," Davey said. "Why won't you tell me?"

"I thought you'd be happy," I told him. "Don't you remember the very end of last summer? That day when I told you I wanted time with her and not you? You cried, but I went anyway."

As I said the words, a sickly feeling wrapped tight around my stomach. Davey and I rarely fought, but we had it out that day. Mrs. Ochoa would say that it was toothpaste squeezed out of the tube—that I couldn't take those words back, no matter how much I wanted to. But I was going to do my best to try.

I swallowed hard. "I could apologize a hundred times and it wouldn't be enough. But I'm sorry, okay?"

He nodded. A welcome breeze curled around us—a moment of relief from the blazing sun. But I didn't feel better. As we walked, guilt settled in my stomach like a sour milkshake.

The afternoon was meltingly hot. By the time we reached the dock, we were covered in sweat. We didn't have to stop at the ticket booth because crew family members rode for free. We boarded along with the crowd and saw Dad's friend Mr. Torres taking tickets. He smiled and waved us through.

"Haven't seen you much this summer—my goodness, you're growing fast," he said. "Visiting your dad today?"

I said yes and Davey nodded shyly. We headed to the bridge and found Dad right away. He was drinking coffee and chatting with some of the other workers.

When he saw us, he beamed. "I didn't know you were coming to visit!"

I exchanged glances with Davey. It was so easy to make Dad happy. Usually we visited him a few times a week, but we'd been too busy lately.

"Surprise!" I said, hugging him.

He pulled back to look at us, eyes twinkling. "Are you going to ride along?"

His smile grew wider when I said yes. We hopped up on the platform where we always sat—best view on the ship. There was always a lot of activity immediately before the ship was underway, so Davey and I stayed in our spots.

"I wanted to ask about your stories," Dad said over his shoulder. "I know you were feeling blocked. Is summer helping?"

Besides Davey, Dad was the only person who understood how important writing was to me. I think it was because he liked to write poems when he could. Usually they were about the ocean or Mom.

I wrinkled my nose. "Still stuck. The words sound great in my head but when I put them on the page, they're suddenly terrible."

Dad nodded sympathetically, patting the pocket where he kept his poetry notebook. "I've been there. Keep trying—the words will come when you're ready."

One of the workers asked Dad a question about one of the controls. He assured us he'd be back to check in at the next stop.

"We need to visit more," I muttered under my breath. "Maybe you should go with him for a shift while I go with Mom to do her research."

Davey seemed to think this over. Eventually, he nodded.

The first leg of the ferry route took about twenty minutes. When we stopped, Dad turned to us.

"Should we wander?"

He grabbed his coffee cup. Davey and I hopped down to follow him.

First, we wandered along the top deck, where people sat to eat snacks or enjoy the view. We stood so we could watch the cars being parked.

Dad leaned against the railing. "That was my first job."

Davey raised his eyebrows at me. I shrugged.

"You never told us that," I said.

Dad smiled. "It requires excellent spatial relations. And lots of patience to deal with people who are particular about their vehicles."

I peered up at him. "Did you like it?"

Dad sighed. "Not really, but being on the water was my dream. I hoped to work my way up to being the ferry master someday."

His dream. I thought of the bridge and how it could take away everything, including the ferryboats. I could tell that Davey was thinking the same thing.

"Did you hear about the bridge they're building?" I asked.

Dad nodded. "It's been in the works for a while."

"But why didn't you ever say anything?"

Dad looked confused, glancing first at Davey and then at me. "It's not a secret—it's been in the news. Mom and I have discussed it many times over the last few months."

I looked out at the water. Maybe it was my fault. I'd been so focused on other things. And I *had* been avoiding the newspaper. But how could I have missed news this big? Usually, I could count on Davey to pay attention to what happened on the island. I guess we'd both been distracted.

Dad scratched his head. "Come on, Bex-Bean. We wouldn't keep it from you on purpose. Ask me anything—I'm an open book."

"What happens if that bridge gets built?" I asked. "Will it shut down the ferryboats? Will you lose your job?"

Dad blew out a deep breath. "That's a *lot* of questions."

Davey looked at him sideways.

I frowned. "You said I could ask anything!"

Dad rubbed the muscles in the back of his neck. "All right. I don't think anyone knows how the bridge will affect our island. I hope the ferryboats won't change much, but I suppose anything could happen. The possibilities are exciting."

I exchanged looks with Davey. *Exciting?* Dad had lived on the island his whole life and he loved it just as much as we did. His response didn't make sense. Davey looked as confused as I felt.

My head was starting to hurt. "Dad, exactly what are you saying?"

Dad took a long drink of his coffee. When he spoke, his voice sounded far-off, almost like he was talking to himself.

"It's true that being on this ferryboat was what I always wanted," he said. "But I'm not the same person I was when I got that first job parking cars. Maybe it wasn't fair to keep Mom here all this time. Originally, she came to Pelican Island for her research. If we lived closer to the university, she would have time for her dreams, too."

My eyes bulged. Davey gave me a can-you-believe-this? look.

"Mom has time for research during the summer. We can't leave. The island is our *home*." My voice caught on the last syllable.

"Sorry I upset you," Dad said, looking back and forth between us. His brown eyes were soft and gentle. "The ferryboats won't change for a long time, if they do at all. I want to make sure that everyone in this family feels like they have a chance at what makes them happy."

I crossed my arms tightly. "Staying here makes me happy."

Davey crossed his arms, too, and nodded emphatically.

"Noted." Dad took off his cap and yawned. He stretched his arms, tilting his chin skyward. I could see the top of his head, where his red hair had begun to thin. When he looked back at us, his eyes crinkled in a grin.

"I better get back to the bridge. If you're planning a trip to the snack bar, do it before we pull into Port Rogers. It's usually a big crowd that boards, especially this time of day." He reached into his pocket and took out a few bills, handing them to me.

I glanced at Davey, who beamed. We would definitely be making a trip to visit Mary Ellen for some extra-large, extra-buttery deliciousness.

I squinted up at Dad. "Why is that stop so busy?"

Dad tapped his coffee mug. "Probably it's because of the attractions. People buy a day pass, hit the aquarium or the art museum, then travel to other islands to shop and visit other beaches."

I pocketed the money. "Thanks, Dad."

He grinned. "Of course. Now, behave, okay? You know I have eyes all over the ship."

That made me laugh. He meant that everyone who worked on the ferry would look out for Davey and me— they'd report back to him if we got into the slightest mischief.

"I promise," I said. Davey saluted.

Dad headed back to the bridge, walking with his long-legged, loping stride. Before he rounded the corner, he whirled back to look at us. He gave a little wave and then disappeared out of sight.

"Let's go see Mary Ellen," I said. "I'm ready for that extra-buttery popcorn."

We waited in line. When she saw us, she beamed and scooped our bucket extra high. We went back to the railing and ate the yellow-soaked pieces one by one. When we arrived in Port Rogers, a crowd was waiting by the dock.

"I guess Dad was right about this being the busiest stop," I said.

Davey frowned slightly, like he was thinking hard. "That's it!"

I sighed. "What?"

"Port Rogers has an *art museum*," Davey said.

I wrinkled my forehead. This wasn't news. I knew for a fact that each of us had gone there on a third-grade field trip.

Davey looked at me semi-patiently. "Bex, *think*."

Sometimes it was annoying having a genius for a little brother.

"I don't get it," I said flatly.

Davey tapped his chin. "What's in an art museum? Let's see. Paintings, pottery, sculptures . . . and statues. Lots and *lots* of statues."

My eyes widened. "You think that someone there might know about our statue? You think they could identify a mark?"

Davey grinned quietly.

Sometimes it was *amazing* having a genius for a little brother.

CHAPTER 14

~~Dear Sir or Ma'am:~~

~~Dear People of the Museum:~~

~~Dear Statue Experts:~~

Davey sighed in exasperation. "Oh, would you let me do it already?"

He grabbed the composition book from me, turned the page dramatically, and began to write. Squish perched in his lap, staring at me with a judgmental look on her face.

To Whom It May Concern:
Recently we discovered what we believe to be an important statue.

Davey paused. "Should I say we found it in the marsh?"
I grimaced. "Definitely not."

We cannot disclose the precise location but it is
somewhere in the general area around Port Rogers.
It was marked with the following symbol:

We were wondering if you had any information about
the artist who may have created this statue.

"We were *wondering?*" I asked. "I know you're trying to
be polite, but this sounds way too relaxed. We need to find
out what it is soon, before the developers flatten it."
"Quit breathing on me." Davey scooted his chair away.
He stuck the end of the pencil in his mouth for a moment,
thinking, and then returned to the letter.

It is a matter of utmost importance and quite urgent.

"Quite?" I asked.
Davey nodded firmly. "Adults say *quite*. They say it
quite a lot, actually, ha ha."
I rolled my eyes, but Davey was already back to
writing.

Most sincerely,
R. D. Wheeler

I squinted at the page. "Who in the world is R. D. Wheeler?"

Davey tapped the letter lightly with his finger. "'R' for Rebecca. 'D' for Davey. 'Wheeler,' because it's our last name."

I shoved him lightly. "Yes, I *know* 'Wheeler' is our last name! But why don't we put Bex and Davey?"

Davey sniffed. "Because it would sound like we're a couple of kids."

"We *are* a couple of kids," I reminded him.

Then it was Davey's turn to roll his eyes. "They won't take it seriously if they think it came from us. We have to sound official, like grown-ups."

He folded the paper neatly into thirds and slid it into an envelope we'd swiped from Mom's desk.

We walked to the mailbox at the end of our driveway. Just before he placed the letter inside, he held it out to me.

"Here, Bex," he said. "Spit on it for luck."

I scowled. "That's disgusting. You're supposed to kiss things for luck, not spit on them."

Davey gagged. "Kissing is *more* disgusting."

I ignored him, dropping the envelope in the mailbox. I didn't like that we were without a backup plan, but I couldn't think of anything else. There was a lot riding on that little letter—it held our only hope of saving The Thumb.

PART THREE
330 days without rain

CHAPTER 15

It wasn't really summer until we lost track of our days, and that's what happened after we mailed the letter.

That's not exactly right. Let me back up and start again.

Of course I checked the mailbox every day to see if we'd heard back. Even our mail carrier commented on it, saying she couldn't remember the last time someone had been so excited to see her.

But I was determined to have a regular summer. We hadn't seen Jocelyn and the builders again. As long as I managed to ignore the orange "X" on our live oak, I could enjoy our time at The Thumb. Like any good writer, I knew how to keep my eyes on the parts that mattered and leave the other stuff behind.

Each morning, I paddled us through the marsh. By the

time we arrived, we'd both be bursting with excitement. As the water lowered, more of the statue was revealed, bit by bit. I was especially fascinated by her expression, which seemed to change when viewed from different angles. Was she kind or angry? Full of joy or sorrow? It seemed to depend on the way I looked at her.

After I'd examined the statue thoroughly, we often sat in the live oak or explored the salt creeks, searching for periwinkle shells and other treasures. Each hour melted gloriously into the next, and we found ourselves in tune with the rush of the tides. We had no use for calendars or watches. Instead, we calibrated to the setting sun, the quiet stillness of a morning, and the elegance of an egret soaring overhead.

Our friends Fritz and Opal, the river otters, returned. They looked sleeker somehow, their coats shinier—but the one we called Fritz had a gash along the side of his head.

"Oh no," I cried when I saw him. "His poor ear." It had been split, giving him a lopsided appearance.

Davey looked curious. "Most animals in the marsh won't tangle with an otter. Maybe it was a bobcat—or even an alligator!"

I shuddered. "Don't say that. I hate the idea of something happening to them."

Davey shrugged. "He's fine, though—look." Together we watched as they playfully ducked in and out of the cordgrass.

"I think they're brother and sister," Davey continued. "They have fun and they're always together. Like you and me."

I didn't know if Fritz and Opal were really siblings, but I could see why Davey thought so. They, too, had extensive conversations in the marsh, among the cordgrass and lying on the sandy shore. Of course, their talk was made up of whistles, buzzes, chirps, and growls. But sometimes siblings have their own secret language. When you truly know someone, words are optional.

CHAPTER 16

One evening, while working at her desk, Mom looked up and asked if I wanted to join her in the kayak the next day. Davey decided it would be good timing for him to ride along with Dad.

The next morning, I woke up to the smell of fresh muffins. Before going downstairs, I peeked in Davey's room. I knew he wouldn't be there—Dad's shift started early—but I still felt a pang when I saw his empty bed. He always kept his room neat, but it seemed tidier than usual, with perfectly pulled-up covers and not a thing out of place. On the shelf I spotted LEGO bricks and the glint of his science fair medals. Mom must have given up the summer clean-out project—at least for the time being.

I padded downstairs. In the kitchen, Mom scooped

kibble into the cat bowl. Ungrateful Squish meowed loudly and swished her tail as if announcing that breakfast was not coming quickly enough. It was hard to live up to her standards.

The bread basket was heaped high with banana muffins. At my spot were sliced strawberries in a pink bowl and a tiny pitcher of cream for me to pour over them.

I wasted no time digging in.

"This is great, Mom, thanks," I told her between mouthfuls.

Mom sipped her tea. "You've been up and out the door so early most mornings. It was nice to make a special breakfast for a change."

After I'd had my fill of breakfast, I leaned back in my chair. "Where will we go today?"

Mom spread a map of the marsh across the kitchen table. Long ago, she had abandoned the official maps for her own versions, which were more detailed and accurate. For her research, she favored an area in the opposite direction of The Thumb. There, the marsh was lined with multiple salt creeks where she could explore and take samples to her heart's content.

Her finger traced the route. "We'll go south, then cut over toward the mainland to take more water and soil samples. I found huge groupings of fiddlers living here. I'm curious about how the drought is affecting them."

Remembering the crabs made me feel a pull toward

the statue, where I'd encountered so many over the past few weeks. I wondered what new parts of the statue had been revealed overnight with the lowering water level.

Something showed in my expression, because Mom peered at me carefully. "Bex? Is there somewhere you'd rather go—maybe out to The Thumb?"

I shook my head. If we passed anywhere nearby, Mom would see the statue and it would ruin everything. I'd have to wait for later this afternoon, when Davey and I could go again.

She rolled up the paper, nodding as if the matter was settled.

"Wear your water sandals with the strap," she said. "At some point, we'll be wading in mud."

Out at the dock, we put in the kayak. The morning mist clung to the water. The gliding of the kayak was almost silent, and Mom and I were quiet as we paddled. I'd spent so much time in the rowboat this summer that it felt odd to be upright as we moved through the water. In the rowboat, it always seemed like I exercised my legs as much as my arms, but in the kayak I could only use my upper body. But still, my muscles were strong and I matched Mom's pace easily.

We stopped near a patch of cordgrass with a sandy shore.

"Look," she murmured.

Hundreds—maybe *thousands*—of fiddler crabs scurried and burrowed in the sand. They were like a carpet with claws and eyes.

"Do you remember how to tell the males and females apart?" Mom asked.

Sometimes she can't leave behind that biology-teacher stuff.

I pointed at one that was about the length of my thumb. "The girls have two small claws, both used for feeding. The boys have one big claw used to defend territory and attract a mate."

When they weren't scrambling, the crabs scooped pluff mud and then put it in their mouth parts. Next, the crab ate bits of animal or plant matter before spitting out the mud in a tiny ball. The females were faster at feeding because they could use both of their claws at the same time. The males, on the other hand, had one normal claw and one that was too big to eat with. I thought that was silly, but Mom said that they needed a way to get girl crabs to notice them.

Mom hopped out of the boat, balancing herself in the slippery muck. In one hand she held her kit for taking samples and in the other she gripped a purple weather-proof notebook. I couldn't help thinking of my black composition book, lonely and neglected back at home. Sometimes I envied Mom's scientific data. It would be easy to fill pages and pages with facts, instead of trying to create a story out of thin air.

Mom clicked her mechanical pencil. "In nature, everything has a purpose. As the crabs eat, they clean and aerate the marsh."

I watched one climb over another. "You said you were worried about them, but they look fine to me."

"Species in the marsh must adapt—they need to handle fresh water, salt water, and the mix of the two. But it's been so long without rain. The salinity levels are higher than they should be."

After Mom took her samples, we continued paddling. The day was getting warmer, and the mist had disappeared. Sweat dripped from my forehead and neck.

We'd been out for a couple of hours when Mom steered us over to a sandbank. She pulled out a bag of muffins and handed me one.

Mom swigged from her water bottle and then wiped her mouth. "How are you doing these days, Bex?"

I swallowed a mouthful of muffin. "Fine."

Mom's eyebrows drew together in concern. "I mean, how are you *really*? Are you lonely? Do you want to invite a friend over? What about Meena or Grace—you haven't mentioned them since the school year ended."

I shook my head. "Meena's family is traveling in Europe this summer. Grace went to sleepaway camp in the mountains."

Mom sighed. "Well, it's a blessing that Millie is back. It seems like you've been having a lot of fun out at The Thumb together. She must love it like you do."

I frowned, about to say, "Millie hasn't been out in the marsh since last summer."

But then I hesitated. I didn't know how to explain that we were no longer friends.

"Yeah. We've been having a lot of fun," I said.

I regretted the words immediately. Lying to Mom wasn't okay. Especially for me. Like any good writer, I considered myself a truth-teller. But the fib had slipped out, as if it had a mind of its own.

Mom beamed. "That's my Bex. I'm so happy to hear that you've been making the most of a difficult summer."

After she said that, I really felt bad. My stomach hurt like I'd been punched.

"Mom?"

She looked at me with her kind blue eyes, so much like Davey's that it sometimes startled me. I gulped.

I was about to say: "Wait."

I was about to say: "Let me back up and start again."

I wanted to spill everything about Millie and the statue—and about how scared I was about possibly losing The Thumb.

But then I saw something move to the left of us. I gasped.

"Mom, look!" There, swimming alongside us, was Opal. Even though most of her body was submerged, I'd recognize that little face anywhere, and her two perfect, rounded ears.

Mom turned her head to look. "I've always loved otters. They have such silly personalities."

I searched the water, expecting another furry head to pop out above the surface—but none did. "Why is she by herself?"

Mom glanced around. "Do you think there are more?"

"I've seen this one at The Thumb," I said. Panic rose in my voice. "But always in a pair. Where's the other? Where's the one she's always with?"

A terrible image appeared in my mind. That gash on the side of Fritz's head, his split ear. What if the same predator had returned for a second try at a meal?

"Do you think it's the same one—all the way out here?" Mom asked doubtfully. "Sometimes it's hard to tell them apart."

Heat flushed my cheeks. My eyes prickled with tears. "I'm positive."

Mom rubbed my back. "They probably separated so they could hunt in different places today."

I shook my head. "I've *never* seen them apart, Mom. Not once this whole summer."

Mom was quiet for a while. Then she cleared her throat. "It's difficult, isn't it? Letting yourself love something in the wild like that. Every little life out here in the marsh is doing its best to survive, but injury and death are part of the deal. It's how the system works."

I scowled, staring out at the water. "Frankly, that system stinks."

Mom was quiet. "It most definitely does," she said finally.

I turned sideways in the kayak so I could see her out of the corner of my eye. "Mom, I know you love the marsh. But Dad said that we might move away so you could be closer to the university. Is that right?"

Mom's eyebrows popped up in surprise. She looked down at her lap, brushing away a few tiny muffin crumbs.

"I—I don't know," she said finally. "I didn't know he was still thinking about that."

I was tired of all their whispered conversations. It seemed that they were making big decisions without even thinking about what was best for Davey and me.

I tightened my arms across my chest. "That's not fair, Mom. Why am I just finding out?"

"Oh, Bex," Mom said softly. "We aren't keeping anything from you. Dad mentioned the idea at the beginning of summer. He's trying to support me—and my research—and make sure I won't have regrets. Living on the mainland would have its advantages—there are things you'd like there. Lots of other kids, more schools, different opportunities."

I felt a pit in my stomach. She reminded me of Jocelyn, trying to sell me on something that I would absolutely hate.

Mom straightened her glasses. "But when it comes down to it, I'm not sure that I could ever leave this place. It would be like leaving a piece of myself behind."

"Yeah," I said. "I know exactly what you mean."

The light glared on the water and hurt my eyes. I wiped at them with the back of my hand.

"I know that I get wrapped up in my research each year," Mom went on. "Sometimes I feel so close to figuring out something big—something important. But being your mom is as important to me—*more* important. It can be tricky to balance it all."

"It's okay," I told her. My voice was scratchy, probably because I needed another drink from the water bottle. "You don't have to choose—you can be a great mom *and* a great researcher."

She pressed my hand. "I hope you know that I'm here whenever you need me. Dad too."

I nodded.

"And again," she added, "I'm so glad you have Millie again this summer. That's a special friendship—it helps to have someone who knows your history so well."

My insides twisted. I told myself that it was a small thing and not worth the trouble to talk about. I didn't want to ruin the moment. Out in the marsh, it was sometimes better to let certain things go.

CHAPTER 17

A few days later, Davey and I headed downtown again. Mom had asked us to pick up some groceries from Mrs. Ochoa's shop, Farm & Field. The store specialized in items that were locally produced, and it was as popular with islanders as it was with tourists.

We were crossing the alley behind Maple Crescent when Davey narrowed his eyes. "What is that?"

On the side of the road was a small, slumped something.

"A cat," Davey said evenly. "It must have been hit by a car."

I shuddered. "It's dead, Davey. Don't look at it."

He walked closer. "I'm going to see if there's a tag."

My heart started beating fast. "Someone else will find it."

Davey folded his arms and stared me down. "Seriously, Bex? If Squish got hurt, I'd want to know."

I didn't want to look, but I couldn't stop myself.

"I hate cars," I muttered. "People drive too fast."

Davey crouched down. "No tag. I can ask Mom or Dad to put it on the neighborhood list."

I wanted to leave, but Davey was still standing there. And then I heard him speak.

"Goodbye, little cat. I am sorry you had to die. I hope it didn't hurt."

Fat tears flooded my eyes, but I wiped them before they could fall. Davey trotted back to me and we continued walking. I couldn't shake the feeling that I'd let him down.

When we reached the store, we stood outside the brick building for a moment. There were bouquets of flowers, kept fresh in buckets of water carefully placed beneath black-and-white-striped awnings. A display of pinwheels spun in the breeze, and the words Farm & Field were painted in gold on a sign that hung above two glass doors.

Inside, we were greeted by a blast of cool air that smelled of lavender and lemons. Mrs. Ochoa was helping a couple with a big basket full of cheeses and meats. The store sold those kits only in tourist season. Islanders would rather pack a simple sandwich, but the visitors squealed over wedges of cheese and the tiny pots of jam. Millie once told me that between the fancy picnics and the freshly churned ice cream, the store made almost all its money during the summer months.

Davey and I walked past a display of sustainably produced granola and turned the corner to the refrigerated case. Mom liked the eggs from Button Creek Farm, and she also wanted avocados and bananas. Davey always remembered to check for bruises and soft spots.

"Maybe we'll have enough left for a cone," I whispered.

I began to do the math in my head—but then something made me forget all about ice cream. Bundled at the end of the aisle was a stack of newspapers. A headline on the front page screamed: "PELICAN ISLAND BRIDGE TO PROVIDE CONNECTIVITY." Smaller words underneath said: "Way to Grow!"

The bridge. The back of my neck got warm. "Come look at this."

We read the article carefully. The proposal for the project had passed its initial round and was approved to start a new phase. That meant the bridge was closer to being built.

My heart drifted to somewhere around my ankles. I didn't know why I was surprised. Ever since we'd learned about the bridge, we seemed to see it everywhere. It was unfair that the project was moving along so quickly. If we could slow it down, Davey and I would have more time to investigate the statue—more time to figure out what to do next.

"Hey there," a teasing voice said. "Did you really think you could come in here without saying hi?"

Mrs. Ochoa held out her arms for a hug and Davey and I crossed to her. Like always, she smelled like vanilla and grapefruit.

She had been our neighbor our entire lives. At some point along the way, she'd become more like a bonus grandma. She always sent little treats our way—like the jams Millie had delivered—and each year at Christmas, she invited Davey and me over for an entire day of cookie baking.

She clasped her hands together. Her fingernails were painted coral and I wondered if Millie had done it for her. She was always good at staying in the lines.

Mrs. Ochoa beamed at us. "I can't get over how tall you are!"

It was one of those things that adults like to say. I'd grown a little that summer but my brother looked the same as he always had.

"It's hot outside—you need some refreshment. A scoop of ice cream? Limeade?" She paused. "Or maybe you're looking for Millie? She's at the beach with a few island kids. I bet she'd love it if you joined them."

I hesitated. It was hard to tell how much Mrs. Ochoa knew. Clearly, she was under the impression that Millie and I were still friends. I didn't want to correct her and have that information get back to Mom.

"Oh, that's right," I said, as if Millie had told me and I'd forgotten. "But Mom needs these groceries."

Mrs. Ochoa glanced at our basket. "Did you find everything?"

I started to answer, but Davey poked me in the side. When I glanced over at him, he nodded at the stack of newspapers.

"What do you think about the plan for the bridge?" I asked.

"It's going to be good for business," Mrs. Ochoa said, returning to her spot behind the counter. "But it's also going to change things around here a lot."

Davey looked at me pleadingly. I could read his expression—I knew he thought we should tell her. I scowled and shook my head. Mrs. Ochoa was great, sure—but she was still an adult.

"Why don't you tell her yourself?" I whispered.

I felt guilty for even thinking this, but sometimes I wished that Davey would talk around other people more often. It wasn't fair that I always needed to handle so much on my own. Besides, I didn't understand why he wanted to bring someone new into our circle. Bex and Davey, Davey and Bex. We didn't need anyone else—not even Mrs. Ochoa.

Davey leaned toward me, his voice pitched low. "She could help."

I raised my eyebrows. Mrs. Ochoa knew everything

that happened within a hundred-mile radius of our island—maybe more. But still, I didn't know if we should involve her. If she got curious about why we were asking, it would be hard to keep the statue secret.

When she began scanning our groceries, Davey stepped on my foot.

"Quit it," I muttered.

Davey shot me a look that said, "Ask her."

I cleared my throat. "Do you think there's anything that might make the plan change?"

She paused. "Like what?"

I scrunched my forehead. "What if they found something important on that side of the island—then would they have to build the bridge somewhere else?"

She smoothed the front of her apron. "I guess it would depend on what it was. What were you imagining?"

"I don't know," I said quickly. "It was only an idea."

Mrs. Ochoa tilted her head at me, her brown eyes shining. "There's no such thing as *only* an idea. Ideas are where everything starts. What do *you* think about the bridge?"

That was the great part about Mrs. Ochoa. She always took the time to listen to our opinions.

I shrugged. "I hadn't heard anything about it, but suddenly it's everywhere."

Mrs. Ochoa passed the bananas over the scanner. "Hmm. It's been in the news for a while. But I know it's been a busy year."

My cheeks warmed. "Well, no one told me."

Mrs. Ochoa patted my hand. She looked at me a little extra long. "Sometimes the heart sees what it wants."

Davey crossed his eyes. I could tell he was thinking, *Adults—they don't always make a lot of sense, but what can you do?*

I pulled away. "We don't need a bridge. Things are fine the way they are."

Mrs. Ochoa nodded and then started packing our items in the bags.

A family with five towheaded kids came in, making a big commotion. Two spun the postcard rack while the others crowded around the ice cream counter.

"Listen, Bex," Mrs. Ochoa said. "I'm here if you ever want to talk. Millie and I are going to make strawberry pie and peppermint popcorn this weekend. Maybe you'd like to join us?"

Before I could answer, she went to scoop the ice cream. But even though I loved Mrs. Ochoa's popcorn and pie, I had no interest in spending time with Millie. Besides, Davey and I had other things we needed to do.

CHAPTER 18

We tried every Internet search term we could think of. We even went to the library and read a book about local art. But eventually, we realized that the letter was our best hope. So we spent most of our time in the live oak at the marsh. Waiting.

Clouds hovered overhead but refused to share even a drop of rain. If I could have reached them, I would have squeezed them like sponges. On the ground below us, Squish stretched out in the shade, napping. If it was too hot for her to hunt for bugs, then it was too hot for most other things as well.

I eyed my black composition book. The gray, over-erased page stared back at me accusingly. Sighing, I slammed it shut.

Davey looked up from his novel, blinking. "What's wrong?"

"The usual," I grumbled. "It's never going to rain. We haven't heard back from the museum. And no matter what I try, I can't write anything decent."

Davey shrugged. "Tell the truth. That's all you have to do."

I slouched against the tree. That was easy for him to say. The real truth meant admitting that I worried about everything: the statue, The Thumb, my writer's block, and Davey's stuck words.

"Let's go home," I said glumly. "The summer is beat down and busted." I swung down from my branch and landed on the sandy shore.

Davey closed his book. "It's not *that* bad."

"And *you*," I said, narrowing my eyes at the statue. It almost seemed like it was laughing at us.

I'd had enough. I got in the boat and Davey and Squish joined me. I rowed forcefully, taking out my anger on the water. What was the use of finding a mysterious statue if a bridge could destroy everything I cared about?

At home, I tied up the boat while Davey danced on the dock.

"Come on," he said. "Let's check the mail."

"I don't know if I care anymore," I said, remembering the statue's smug expression.

Davey stopped still. "You don't mean that. Come on."

I sighed but went along with him. When I opened the mailbox, there was a stack of junk mail. But underneath was a white envelope addressed to R. D. Wheeler.

My hands started shaking. I held it up.

"Open it, open it!" he cried.

Right there, I ripped it open. Davey crowded close so he could read, too.

PORT ROGERS ART MUSEUM

Dear R. D. Wheeler,

We thank you most sincerely for your letter. It is always a pleasure to hear from someone who has a great interest in art, and the idea of a mystery to be solved is quite exciting indeed.

Without examining the artifact in person, it would be difficult if not impossible to make an accurate assessment. We regret that we do not have an exact match in our system that directly indicates who the artist may have been.

However, we noted that there is a resemblance to the following mark, which is associated with the reclusive and brilliant Effie Framingham:

Effie Framingham lived in and around the Port Rogers area for many decades. Her early works were sculpture, primarily casting statues from bronze. Later in her years, she focused on temporary art. Many of her works explored themes of nature and loss.

Her whereabouts have been unknown for upward of twenty years.

We are very excited to view the artifact and determine whether this is a previously undiscovered work of Effie Framingham. Coincidentally, we are about to open an exhibit of her works. We would love for you to attend and share more about the artifact you located.

I have enclosed two tickets to the opening exhibition, which will be held in one week's time. Several experts on Effie Framingham's work will be in attendance. Although we would not be in a position to confirm the authenticity of your artifact, we are confident that our staff could provide an initial assessment and assist in deciding any future steps.

Thank you again for contacting us. We do hope to see you at the opening.

Sincerely,
Lali Rao
Public Relations
Port Rogers Art Museum

I read the letter three times, trying to understand.

"What's 'reclusive'?" I asked.

Davey's forehead scrunched. "It means staying away from others—living far away from them. That explains why they don't know if she's alive—no one has heard from her in a long time."

I looked at the mark. "It's not exactly like the one on the statue, but it's similar."

Davey studied the page closely before answering. "It's impossible to tell for sure. *They* aren't certain, and they're the experts."

My shoulders slumped. I was sure that the letter would bring us answers, but it only gave us more questions. All the curiosity and excitement that had built up over the weeks escaped from me in a shudder, like air from a deflating balloon.

Davey frowned. "Don't get discouraged, Bex. Maybe the people at the museum can help. We need to find a way to get there for the exhibit opening."

I raised my eyebrows.

"Go to Port Rogers without Mom and Dad knowing? It's not that easy. We'd be recognized the minute we stepped on the ferryboat." Our parents were okay with salt-marsh exploration, but that was in our backyard. Traveling to a big city alone would be out of the question.

Davey sighed. "Maybe it's time to share it with them, Bex. They'll be on our side."

I let myself imagine telling our parents. They'd definitely want to know more. Mom would call someone in the art department at her old university. Dad would visit one of the island old-timers to see if they remembered anything about a statue. It would become a family project—the whole island might get involved.

But it wouldn't belong to Davey and me anymore. We were close to figuring it out. I could feel it.

"Not yet," I said. "Just one more week. If we don't learn anything at the museum, we'll tell them then."

Davey watched quietly as I stuffed the letter in my back pocket. I could tell that he didn't agree, but he could compromise—and that was something.

All we needed was a plan.

CHAPTER 19

Davey and I sat high in the live oak.

That morning, Squish had hidden in the shade under the porch when we were getting in the rowboat. I was beginning to think she had the right idea. It was too hot to read, too hot to talk, and even too hot to *think*, which was unfortunate—because the special exhibit was a few days away, and Davey and I still didn't have a plan.

Davey handed me a yellow M&M. "Read what you have so far."

I popped the candy in my mouth and let the candy shell melt. Usually I adored the taste, but that day it was too sticky-sweet. I swallowed hard. It was a bad day indeed when chocolate didn't taste good.

Sighing, I held up the composition book. Even from a distance, Davey could see that I'd written *THE PLAN* in thick pencil. The rest of the page was blank. Getting off the island was the tricky part. Not that I would ever admit it, but it was one time when the bridge would have come in handy.

"We could row to the mainland and then take a cab," Davey suggested.

I shook my head. "That would cost a gazillion dollars."

Davey frowned at the water. "We could ask Mrs. Ochoa or Mr. Harris to help. We could say we had an appointment."

I blew out a deep breath. "They'd tell Mom and Dad immediately."

Davey was quiet. I lay on my back, gazing through the branches at a patch of faded-blue-jeans sky.

"Why won't it rain already?" I asked for the thousandth time.

"I wish there was a way for us to take the ferryboat," Davey said stubbornly, ignoring me.

I balled up my fists and pressed them against my eyes. "We'd be recognized the second we stepped on board. Maybe even before that."

Davey traced his fingers on the bark's bumpy ridges. When he spoke, the words came slowly.

"What if . . . what if we told Dad we were exploring the ship? Then we'd sneak off at Port Rogers, go to the museum, and get back the next time the ship was back at the dock."

I shook my head. "What if he decided to look for us

when we were gone? Besides, the crew would never let us leave without Dad."

He rubbed the sides of his head, like his brain was exhausted. In the distance, a heron squawked its *roh-roh-roh* call. I fanned myself with my hand. We needed an idea, but ours were all dried up.

Davey rolled sideways on the wide branch and peered through the leaves. Then he gasped, craning his neck to look at the water.

"What is it?" I asked.

He pointed. "The otters!"

My breath caught in my throat. I didn't believe it could be true, but Fritz and Opal were back, darting through the water like shadows. Tears squeezed in my eyes. I'd been so worried about Fritz, but he was perfectly fine— with his sister, like always.

As we watched, they ducked completely under the surface. Davey and I leaned forward to see where they would pop up. Eventually, bubbles appeared near the statue.

One emerged from the water and onto the bank, a crab tucked in its paws.

"There! That's Opal," I said.

As I spoke, Fritz joined her on the bank, his torn ear flapping. He bumped into her, reaching for the crab, but Opal shouldered him away. Fritz tried again but changed his mind when she scolded him firmly.

Davey raised his voice over Opal's chittering sounds.

"Aw, she won't share. She sure is giving him a piece of her mind."

"Good for her!" I said. "She did the work and he wants to swipe her supper!"

Fritz realized he had to take matters into his own paws, so he splashed back into the water. Soon enough, he emerged with a crab of his own. He scrambled onto the bank, a good distance from Opal, and began to gobble up his meal.

Davey shuddered. *"Yuck!"*

"Oh, hush," I told him. "I've seen you at a seafood boil—you somehow manage to eat your entire body weight in shrimp, crab, and corn."

"None of it is alive and moving when I do," Davey said primly.

The otters must have been famished. They dived and hunted again and again. Finally, they filled their bellies and then rested in a shady patch of cordgrass.

Davey leaned back against his branch, eyelids closing. I felt like I could nap, too, if it weren't for the blank pages of my composition book staring at me accusingly. *You haven't earned a rest*, they seemed to say. *Not until you come up with a plan.*

I swung my legs, looking out at the water. "They looked so different when they hunted—like assassins! I barely recognized them."

Davey's eyes popped open. "Bex . . . that's it!"

I squinted at him. "That's *what?*"

"We'll wear disguises on the ferry," Davey said, sitting upright.

"Like wigs and costumes? This isn't a detective show."

He waved his arms excitedly. "We don't have to wear wigs. We just have to look like tourist kids—not like Davey and Bex. We'll wear sunglasses and hats. If we board separately, they won't realize it's us."

The more I thought, the more I liked it. Taking the ferry made perfect sense. We'd be able to return before anyone noticed we were gone.

My little brother, the genius, had thought up the perfect plan. We just had to make it happen.

PART FOUR

342 days without rain

CHAPTER 20

The minutes crawled by like they were torturing us on purpose.

The day before the exhibition, we didn't go to the marsh at all. Davey and I sat in our backyard under the shade of the big magnolia. A glossy leaf lay on the grass and I shredded it idly. Meanwhile, Davey studied the ferryboat schedule, even though I was certain he'd already memorized it.

The back door of Mrs. Ochoa's house swung open and Millie stormed out. She beelined in our direction and stood there, arms crossed.

"Bex, I need to talk to you."

I looked at her levelly. "Okay."

"Your mom told my grandma she was happy that we spend so much time together," Millie said. "Which is a flat-out lie. Which, honestly, is not a Bex Wheeler thing to do. So I want to know: number one, why are you lying? And number two, where have you been all summer?"

A flame of anger sparked in my chest. Millie didn't get to accuse me of being a liar. "I don't have to tell you anything," I said through clenched teeth.

Millie stomped her foot. "Yes you do! Or . . . or . . . or I'll tell your parents!"

I gasped. This was low. I couldn't let Millie mess up our plans—not when we were so close to finding out where our statue had come from.

"Well?" Millie asked. "Are you going to say something or are you going to stare at me?"

I raised my right eyebrow. "Your grandma *also* thinks we're still hanging out together. What have *you* been up to?"

Millie tucked a piece of hair behind her ear, looking flustered. "Nothing secret."

I rolled my eyes. "Oh, sure. Who's lying now?"

Davey shifted uncomfortably. Tension made him nervous. I pushed my leaf pile toward him.

Millie glanced in his direction before turning her eyes back to me. "It isn't like I'm keeping anything from my grandma. I didn't want her to worry or try to make us be friends again. I've been hanging out with Angelina."

I made a face. Angelina was one of the meanest kids in my entire grade.

Millie sighed. "She isn't *that* bad. Besides, I would rather hang out with you, except you haven't wanted to be friends. I'm worried about you, Bex."

My cheeks flushed. Millie was only three months older than I was, but she was acting like an adult. "You don't need to *worry* about me!"

Millie frowned. "Oh, yes I do!" She was almost shouting. If I didn't act fast, Mom or Mrs. Ochoa would overhear her.

"No," I said, suddenly tired. "You really don't."

Millie put her hands on her hips. "I miss the old Bex. The one who likes green Popsicles best, just like me—even though *no one* likes green Popsicles. The one who writes the best stories and is ruthless in water-balloon fights. The Bex who, no matter what, one hundred percent *always* tells the truth."

Something caught in my throat when she said that. Millie knew me from before my relationship with the truth got complicated. I looked sideways at Davey, who'd arranged the leaf pieces in a neat pile. He turned his hands palm up as if to say, "If it were up to me, we would have told her about the statue a long time ago."

He was right. It was better to let Millie know. If I didn't, Mom or Mrs. Ochoa would find out, and that would risk everything.

I rubbed at the sides of my head. "I'll tell you if you promise to stop yelling."

Millie sat next to Davey. I explained everything—finding the statue, learning about the bridge, receiving the letter, and planning the trip to Port Rogers. If I left out the slightest detail, Davey's sharp elbow dug into my ribs.

After all the words spilled out, I breathed deep. It actually felt good to tell someone.

"So that's the plan," I said. "We'll find out more at the art museum."

A smile spread across her face. "You want me to go with you?"

Something in me tightened and pulled back. I glanced at Davey, who tilted his head thoughtfully. He probably wanted to let her tag along.

I gave him a look. Davey and I were the ones to find the statue. We would be the ones to see it through.

I shook my head. "No thanks."

Millie peered at me, squinting. "But you said—"

"No," I said firmly.

Millie flinched, like the word had hurt her. My stomach squeezed. I didn't want to upset Millie. She might not exactly be my friend anymore, but we had a lot of history together. And I had to admit that it was good to talk to her, even if it wasn't the same as before.

"I'll tell you about it after, though," I said. "Over green Popsicles."

Millie grinned widely. "Promise?"

I let myself smile back. It wasn't such a bad thing, really, to be nice.

Millie touched her earrings, which glinted in the afternoon sunlight. "What exactly are you expecting to find at the museum? Wouldn't it be easier to use the Internet?"

I squinted at her. Did she think we hadn't tried that? We'd done searches after finding the statue and again after getting Effie's name from the museum. Unfortunately, the results were disappointing.

"Except for a few grainy photos, there wasn't much," I said. "She hasn't done any art for a long time, so I guess that's why. So I'm hoping that we'll see one of her old pieces and it will somehow connect to this statue. After we confirm that it's her, we can stop the bridge," I said.

Millie bit her lip. "Would they *really* stop the entire project because of a random piece of art? There's probably a law against dumping things in the marsh. What if it's hurting the environment somehow?"

I took in a sharp breath. Davey's eyes rounded and I knew he was as shocked as I was. Deep in my heart, I knew the statue wasn't hurting anything. But maybe other people wouldn't feel that way.

"That's even more of a reason to talk to people at the museum," I said. "If official art experts get involved, they can stop the bridge."

Millie nodded, but I still felt unsettled. I looked at Davey, whose shoulders had slumped. We needed a boost. I rummaged in his backpack and held up the M&M's. I tossed one to Davey and then held out one to Millie.

She looked surprised to see the candy—but then she

grinned and held out her hand. "You still have the jar. I guess some things never change."

"Of course."

As I let it melt on my tongue, I thought more about the idea of the statue being in the museum. At least it would be safe there. But I couldn't shake the idea that it was supposed to stay in the marsh. I had to find a way to protect it.

Suddenly, Millie looked up. "Wait here."

She raced inside. When she returned, she held a bundle of clothing under her arm. "If you want to blend in, you should wear this stuff. I didn't know what size, so I brought a few choices."

It was a bunch of Pelican Island T-shirts and sweatshirts and bucket hats with embroidered birds and sea creatures on them.

"Are these from the store? Won't your grandma know they're missing?"

Millie shook her head. "This is her donation pile. Most of them are irregular—with uneven stitching or faded lettering. If you give them back when you're finished, she'll never know they were gone."

Millie was being so nice to us, when I hadn't wanted anything to do with her the entire summer. Guilt weighed down my insides.

"Thanks, Millie," I told her. "These are perfect."

Millie hesitated for a moment. "Are you *sure* you don't want me to come along? You shouldn't go by yourself."

"No," I said sharply. Millie's eyes widened. She didn't understand that we would be just fine without her.

Davey shot me a look that said, "Don't be mean."

I cleared my throat. "Sorry, but it's better this way. After the boat gets to Port Rogers, the museum is a short walk away. It's fine."

Millie looked unsure.

"But seriously," I continued. "Thank you for the clothes."

Mille stood up, brushing bits of grass from her shorts. "I better get back—I'm supposed to be helping my grandma in the kitchen."

We watched as she went back inside. Millie wasn't my friend again—not really. Still, it felt good to talk things over with her. She'd known me long enough to understand that if I thought something was important, it was probably worth doing. With her help, we would ride on the ferryboat undetected.

Davey sorted through the pile. He put a tie-dyed hat with a sea turtle on his head. "What do you think?"

I shook my head. "You look pretty silly."

Davey crossed his eyes and stuck out his tongue. "Well, I happen to like it."

We stuffed Davey's red backpack full of Millie's clothes. We were one step closer to making our plan a reality, and I couldn't wait to see what would happen next.

CHAPTER 21

The morning of our trip to the museum, I woke up when it was still dark.

Salt air breezed through my open window and I breathed deep. Part of me wanted to hop out of bed and start getting ready. But before I could push back the covers, I remembered what Davey had said the night before. *Don't dream of going downstairs one minute before eight a.m. If you're up early, Mom will be suspicious.*

Groaning, I rolled onto my back and stared at the ceiling, going over the details of the day in my mind once more. We knew that we couldn't leave the *True Blue* at our dock—Mom might wonder where we'd gone without it. So our plan was to take the rowboat as we always did, but instead of heading toward The Thumb, we'd go toward the side of the island where the ferryboat docked.

After stashing the boat, we'd put on the borrowed clothes and then take the ferry to Port Rogers. What could go wrong?

Only a million things along the way. My main worry was bumping into someone we knew while we were decked out in our tourist outfits. From one look, they'd know we were up to something. Islanders never wore those kinds of clothes, which was why they made such good disguises. Luckily, Davey and I knew the longcut through the alleys and backyards and empty lots. We could make it all the way to town without setting foot on a sidewalk.

Finally, the pale light outside turned golden. I checked my clock and decided that 7:59 would have to be close enough.

Downstairs, Mom leaned against the kitchen counter and sipped her tea. Davey sat at the kitchen table, holding Squish on his lap.

"Good morning," Mom said. "Are you hungry? I could whip up a batch of French toast."

My stomach rumbled, but when I glanced at Davey, he silently shook his head. On a normal day, I would have been excited about a special breakfast. But there was nothing normal about today. We didn't want to do anything that would make Mom stick around any longer than she usually did.

"I think I'll have cereal," I said.

Mom's eyes turned down a bit, like she was disappointed.

I ignored the jumpy butterflies in my stomach and plastered on a smile. "Another time?"

She hugged me, kissing the top of my head. "Of course. How about we go out to lunch instead? We could try that new place downtown that serves bubble tea."

Davey froze, his eyes rounded. We'd never be back in time for lunch.

Mom paused, seeing our hesitation. "Or dinner?"

I breathed out. "That sounds great."

At the table, Davey vibrated with energy, like he might bounce right out of his chair at any moment. We chewed our cornflakes quietly and waited for Mom to leave. For some reason, she lingered that day—asking about how the summer was going, updating us on the fiddler crabs on the other side of the marsh, and wondering aloud about when we would finally see rain.

Davey answered with his usual nods and shrugs, and I kept my answers short as well.

"If she doesn't leave soon, we'll miss the ferry," he muttered.

I gritted my teeth. We wanted to make the earlier boat because Dad wasn't on that one. I was pretty sure our plan would work but not confident enough to test it out anywhere Dad might spot us.

Finally, Mom rinsed her mug in the sink. She blew us kisses and left, the screen door clacking shut behind her.

Davey jumped up to watch through the window and I

followed. After she launched her kayak in the water and paddled out of sight, he turned to me with a grin. "We're in the clear, Bex!"

The minute we stepped outside, I knew it would be a hot day. Once we were in the *True Blue*, I cut through the water as quickly as I could. We arrived at Mooney Park right on schedule and luckily no one was there. Carefully, we pulled the rowboat onto the shore, placing it behind some bushes. It could be seen from the water, if someone was looking—but not from land.

We pulled the tourist clothes over our regular shirts. Davey wore the same silly turtle hat as before. I headed toward our usual longcut that wound through neighborhood houses.

Davey checked his watch. "Sea Salt Boulevard is more direct."

"No," I said.

"But we'll get there so much faster," he said.

"I don't like going that way," I said. "Besides, if someone spots us, then it will mess up the plan."

Davey didn't look happy, but he followed me. At the ticket booth, there was a long line of people waiting to board. A huge group of kids lined up in pairs, likely part of an overnight camp trip to the beach. Counselors called names and made check marks on their clipboards.

My heart pounded. This was one of the trickiest parts of the plan. I'd have to be up close with whoever was selling the tickets. But when I approached the counter, I was relieved to see Holden E. working— a college student with a wide smile who had been hired just a few weeks ago. I'd only met him once before. There was no way he would recognize me.

I shoved the money across the counter.

"Better hurry," he said without looking up. "They're boarding."

When I returned, Davey nodded at a family in line. There were two dads—one was with round glasses and the other with a blue baseball cap and a dark-brown beard. The bearded one held a preschooler who was carrying a toy sailboat and singing at the top of his lungs. The other dad tried to entertain a little girl in the stroller by giving her Cheerios. She scowled at him, alternately dropping them on the ground or cramming them into her mouth by the fistful.

"They're busy enough that they won't notice me," Davey said. "I'll board with them. You get on with that camp group."

This was part of the plan. We knew that we would be harder to recognize with the clothes Millie gave us. But it seemed safest to stay apart until we were off the ferryboat. If we boarded together, it might make someone wonder why two kids were traveling alone.

"All right," I said. "When we disembark in Port Rogers, go to the clock across from the museum. I'll wait for you there."

Davey grinned. "Not if I get there first."

He pressed something in my hand—a yellow M&M. He sidled over to the family and blended in perfectly. Somehow, he managed to stand close enough that an observer would assume they were together—but not so close as to be noticed by either of the dads.

When I handed over my ticket, I ducked my head. Then I found a seat near the camp group. I kept an eye on Davey—impossible to miss in the tie-dyed hat and his red backpack. He flashed me a grin and pointed at his hat. "Do you think Millie will let me keep this?" he mouthed. I held back a laugh and turned away, not wanting to blow our cover.

Usually, the ferryboat was like a second home to us— but that day, I couldn't relax. At any moment, one of the crew might spot us and ask why we were there—or worse, tell Dad.

The journey to Port Rogers seemed slower than usual. When we arrived, Davey and I disembarked separately. A group of senior citizens streamed from a bus. I stepped to the side so they could pass. Davey leaned against the clock casually, waiting for me.

"Told you I'd get here first." Davey looked pleased with himself. He held out his backpack so I could put my sunglasses and hat inside.

"I can't believe the plan worked," I said.

Davey raised his eyebrows. "*I* can't believe you thought it wouldn't."

We looked at the museum—a three-story building made of sand-colored stone. Steps led to the front door, which was surrounded by columns. Purple banners fluttered out front, reading *Ephemera: The Works of Effie Framingham*. My stomach buzzed with excitement.

Davey reached over and punched my arm softly. He was grinning. I took a deep breath. This was where we were going to find out if the statue was hers. This was where we found out if everything we worked on this summer was going to come to anything. This was it.

CHAPTER 22

For a building that looked downright plain on the outside, the inside was a lot more interesting. I had a hazy memory of this from my third-grade field trip, but somehow it was more dazzling than I had remembered.

All the walls were white and the ceilings arched high above our heads. On one side was an enormous skylight that poured so much light into the room that it seemed to glow. In front of us, an elaborate staircase curled into a Y shape—one flight of steps went straight up; then it split in two different directions.

A long line of people stood at the ticket counter. Finally, one of the ticket agents waved us over—her name tag said Claire. Her dark hair shone and she wore eyeglasses the color of raspberry ice cream.

"Good morning," Claire said, taking the tickets from us. If she was surprised to see kids at the museum without any grown-ups, she didn't let on. Instead, she flipped open a brochure and showed us the map, giving us a quick orientation as to where everything was—snack bar, bathrooms, the outer gardens.

She handed me the brochure. "Would you like some recommendations? I'm a big fan of our Egyptian collection. And armor is on the fourth floor."

I liked how she talked to us—she took us seriously, even though we didn't have an adult with us.

"We're here for the special exhibit," I said.

Claire's eyes lit up. "*Ephemera*? Oh, that's so exciting that you're here for the opening day. It's special—I've never seen anything like it."

She explained how to reach the third floor and suggested that we return if we needed more ideas about what to see. Then she began to help the next people in line.

Davey and I walked past the desk, toward the back of the room.

"Elevator or stairs?" Davey asked.

Before I could answer, a haughty voice came from behind us. "Pardon me. You're in the way."

We turned to look. The speaker was a tall woman, with long arms and legs and sharp angles in her face. Her clothes were not summery—they were black and seemed like the kind of thing a spider would wear. Her eyes hid behind sunglasses, but we could definitely see her sneer. She looked at us like we were pieces of gum stuck to her shoe.

I grabbed Davey's arm and we stepped aside.

"Sorry," I said.

She sniffed loudly and swooped onto the elevator. She pressed the button like it owed her a favor.

Davey looked at me with wide eyes.

"Definitely taking the stairs," I muttered.

Our footsteps echoed on the marble steps and we ran our hands over the smooth, polished wood railings. Davey's backpack bounced on his skinny shoulders as he hurried in front of me. My heart felt like it was bouncing, too.

When we reached the hall, a banner said:

EPHEMERA

That which exists for a short time.

"Eff-em-ur-uh," Davey said slowly, studying the sign.

I shook my head. Museums are supposed to be all about what's permanent—normal art like painting, photography, and pottery is designed to last a really long time. Even the sculptures out in the garden feel like they will exist forever, no matter the weather. I wanted The Thumb to last forever, too. Was that too much to ask?

People crowded the entrance—mostly the senior citizens from the bus. But there were younger people, like college students, there, too, and even a few people with baby strollers. But the biggest thing I noticed was the statues. One was at least twenty feet tall. Another hung from the ceiling. On the far side of the room was a display of photographs and videos.

Nearby stood a raised platform with an army of miniature statues no bigger than my thumbnail. From a distance, they didn't look like much. But a description posted nearby explained that each one was unique. A magnifying glass was mounted on a track, and those who wanted a better view could slide it in front of each figure. Davey operated it for a while.

"Look." He pointed the magnifier at a tiny person wearing skis and holding a bunny under one arm. Davey found a ballet dancer with a snorkel, a carpenter wearing a frilly dress, and an astronaut holding a slice of birthday cake.

I craned my neck, searching for the familiar EF symbol. "Do you see any marks on them?"

Davey shook his head. "Not yet."

I sighed. The whole thing seemed pointless, but Davey was content to keep checking each of the figurines, one by one. None of them looked like our statue in the swamp—not exactly. Something about them seemed familiar—the angle of the arms on one, the detail on the clothing on another—but maybe that was just wishful thinking.

I squinted at them. "I don't get it. It would be easier to make them all the same. Or to build a big one so people could see it without a magnifier."

Davey shrugged. "I like them. They're interesting."

We moved on to a larger statue that showed the EF mark on a sash. It didn't look like the letters on our statue—this mark was contained in a circle, identical to the one sent in the letter. I was discouraged. It was starting to feel like we would never have any answers.

"At least it was on the statue's clothing, just like ours was on the belt," Davey said. "That's a good sign."

That was my brother, relentlessly optimistic. We moved from exhibit to exhibit, seeing more of the official EF symbols but nothing that resembled the EF on our statue. Then we reached the section with photographs and videos.

Davey's forehead wrinkled. "What *is* this?"

EPHEMERA

Later in Framingham's career, she began to explore ephemeral art, which is defined as art that is temporary, perishable, or transitory. She was inspired by the use of natural materials in and around the Port Rogers area. During this time, themes of grief and loss are almost constant in her work. Due to the nature of ephemeral art, some of the collection consists of reproductions as well as photographic and video recordings.

We walked under an arch made up of twisting seashells, seaweed, and driftwood. There were photographs showing sculptures that seemed to defy the concept of gravity.

The sign explained that these works were part of a

collection called *Turning Tides*. One had large logs balanced on a delicate tower of shells. Another consisted of stacks of perfectly rounded spheres made of shells and sand.

I studied the text on the wall. "Except for the first one, most of these are copies. The originals were washed into the ocean. She purposely put them near the water because she wanted them to be destroyed. Isn't that weird?"

From behind me, I heard another sniff. It was the spiderlike woman we'd seen in the lobby. She turned and swooshed away.

I looked at Davey and shrugged. Maybe she had allergies. We continued walking, looking at photographs. They showed the way the tide came in and crashed into the sculptures, eventually washing the materials out to sea.

Davey read the sign and then turned toward me. "These works used only natural materials. The original project, the arch at the beginning, she constructed with glue. That's the only reason it still exists—she didn't want to put it back into the environment because the glue part wasn't from nature."

I raised my eyebrows. "If you say so."

When we rounded the corner, I saw something that stopped me in my tracks.

"I know where this is," I said. "This is the beach on Pelican Island. You can see the edge of the visitors' center in this one."

Davey's eyes widened. "That's a good sign, Bex. That means we have proof that Effie Framingham visited our island and made art there."

"Maybe," I said, not wanting to get my hopes up. Lots of people visited. It didn't mean that they left statues behind.

We moved on to the next piece. A nearby sign stated that it was a replica of one of Effie's original works. It was a dining room table set with patterned china, sparkling crystal, and a floral tablecloth, like our grandma might do on a very special occasion. The silverware glinted. The glasses were filled. But the food on the plates was moldy. An acrylic box fit over the table, which allowed us to see the food without experiencing the smell. But looking at the rotten dinner turned my stomach.

An elderly couple stood nearby. The man had about two strands of gray hair on his bald head. His eyebrows were drawn together like two fuzzy caterpillars and he had a rolled-up newspaper tucked under his arm. He rubbed his chin thoughtfully. "For the life of me, I can't see how this qualifies as art, Wilma."

The woman shook her head, her turquoise earrings swinging from side to side. "Keep an open mind, Maurice. Art isn't always pretty."

Maurice scratched his head. "I just don't know."

"You don't have to *know*," she drawled. "As long as it's making you see the world differently, then it's doing its job. I can see by the look on your face that you'll be thinking about it for a while. I'd say we got our money's worth."

Maurice turned toward her, eyes twinkling. "How did you get so smart?"

She murmured something back, but I couldn't hear her words. Hand in hand, they moved along.

I poked Davey in the side. "For the record, I'm with Maurice. I don't get the point."

"Art should make you think or feel," said Davey. "This does both."

I scowled. "But what does it mean?"

Davey shrugged. "It shows the passage of time. That's interesting."

"That's *depressing*, you mean," I said.

"Not to me," Davey said mildly, which I found irritating.

I squinted at him. "Her sculptures aren't bad. But putrid food? Glorified sandcastles? Why? It all feels like a waste."

Davey tilted his head. "There are some things you can't hold on to, I guess."

I rolled my eyes. Another genius moment that I couldn't relate to. As we continued through the exhibit, my patience wore down faster than a stubby pencil eraser. Some parts were interesting—I liked the intricate spirals of sand, the towering piles of stone, and the ice that had been sculpted and stacked in a way that reminded me of stalagmites in a cave. But I didn't understand the meaning.

It was maddening to feel like the answer was just out of reach.

Davey stood in front of a video. First, the screen was dark. Then it showed sand. Then it showed a time-lapse photography of someone—Effie Framingham herself, I guess—creating intricate patterns on top of the sand. First she smoothed out the area so it was completely flat. Then she walked in careful circles, mounding the sand behind her. Every few steps, she took out a brush and scraped the sand to erase her footprints. It looked complicated and painstaking. And pointless.

"Look how careful she is," Davey murmured.

"Now the tide will wash it away. Fabulous," I said flatly.

"Shh," Davey answered.

I sighed. On-screen, the pattern continued to form. Davey was mesmerized.

"Come on," I said. "Let's keep moving."

"Wait," Davey said in a stubborn voice. I knew from experience he wouldn't budge until he was good and ready. I gazed around the hall, trying to decide where to go next. It looked like a choice between more videos about dirt and sticks or a handful of statues that we hadn't seen yet.

I had a sinking feeling in my stomach. All this work— all this *hope*—and it was for absolutely nothing. We were no closer to identifying the statue. We were no closer to saving The Thumb. This summer was turning out to be one big waste. We might as well give up.

Then Davey pulled at my sleeve.

"Bex," he breathed. "Look."

There on the screen in front of us was a pattern of concentric circles. A *familiar* pattern of circles. Davey rummaged in the red backpack and then pulled out the black composition book. He flipped to the page where I'd drawn the design that day, the one that showed the statue's grooves where the algae had settled.

It was exactly the same.

CHAPTER 23

I glanced back and forth between the screen and the composition book.

"You did it, Davey," I whispered.

Davey beamed. "We did it—together. It's her! It has to be."

I looked around us, newly energized. Suddenly, all the art was dazzling, full of possibilities. Any one of these pieces might unlock a clue about Effie Framingham. If we could somehow find her, maybe she would help us talk to the county about the bridge. With her help, we'd be able to save The Thumb.

Davey's face was scrunched, like he was thinking hard. "What if she's dead?"

I glared at him. "Don't *say* that."

He shrugged. "She's old. The letter said her whereabouts are unknown. That might mean dead." He bugged his eyes out and pantomimed a slicing motion near his throat.

I poked him in the ribs. "Let's circle back to the beginning. We already know that she did at least the statue on Pelican Island and the piece by the visitors' center. Maybe there's a clue to tell us where she might be living."

We wandered through the exhibit a second time. But with each step, my shoulders slumped lower. If there were any hints, we were missing them. By the time we got to the end of the hall, Davey looked frazzled.

"Let's take a break," I said. "We'll come back later." As if to agree, my stomach rumbled. I groaned, remembering. "I was going to bring Davey sandwiches."

"They would have gotten smushed anyhow." He reached into his backpack and began to fish around. He handed me three crumpled bills. "Snack bar, east wing, second floor, past Modern and Contemporary."

I was grateful that one of us read maps and, apparently, memorized them. At the café, every table was full. I saw several people from earlier in the day, including Maurice and Wilma sitting together, eating quiche and completing a crossword in ink.

When we reached the front of the line, I ordered a bagel and a large lemonade with two straws. It wasn't much of a lunch—nowhere near as good as the combination of almond butter, bananas, raspberry jam, and potato chips. But it would have to do.

Davey nudged me. "Where should we sit?"

"Let's go to the garden," I said.

We pushed open the double doors and walked outside. It was massive—cool and shady, with tall trees and wide, grassy areas encircling a bubbling fountain. Tables and chairs were arranged on a brick patio, but we opted for a bench underneath a live oak tree. Across from us was a statue of a girl and boy holding hands. I tore the bagel apart and handed half to Davey.

We chewed quietly. There were only a few other people out in the garden—a person with pink hair and a baby stroller, two men with museum name tags having a lunch break, and— Oh. The person from the lobby. I elbowed Davey, but he had already noticed her.

She carried a large cup of coffee and strode toward the fountain, looking around like she was choosing the best seat. When she finally sat, she arranged herself with a flounce. Over her shoulders, she wore a creation that was part scarf and part cape, held together with a silver clasp.

We watched as she rummaged in her handbag and pulled out a spiral-bound pad. She flipped a few pages and began to draw. Being an artist must be nice. She didn't have to wait for words to come—she simply sketched what was in front of her. I thought of my almost-empty composition book. This whole summer hadn't amounted to much.

Next to me, Davey craned his neck. "What's she up to? I think we should find out."

I took a long drink of lemonade and then wiped my mouth. "Go right ahead."

Davey bit his lip. "No, you do it."

Sighing, I crumpled the bag that held our bagel and walked to the trash can on the other side of the garden. Quietly, I made my way toward her. Even though this hadn't been my idea, I was curious about her drawing. I couldn't say why—maybe because it was nice to see someone making regular, normal art after the morning of looking at disgusting food and random seashells.

I crept carefully behind the fountain, finally close enough to peek over her shoulder. She'd sketched the beginnings of the fountain. Clearly, she was talented—even with a few rough pencil lines, the water had a splashy look to it. My eyes wandered to the previous page, where there was a completed drawing. It was the figure of a girl standing near the ocean. The initials in the corner caught my eye, but I couldn't quite make them out. I moved closer.

Suddenly, the woman spun around. She pulled off her sunglasses and glowered at me.

"And who might you be?" she asked.

She slammed the pad of paper shut. But before she did, I caught a glimpse of those initials in the corner. *EF*, it said, written like the mark on the statue.

I was standing in front of the one and only Effie Framingham.

CHAPTER 24

We'd spent so much time waiting and wondering. It seemed impossible that the answer to the mystery was in front of me.

I'd barely blinked before Davey was by my side. There had never been a more loyal brother anywhere in the history of the world.

"I know who you are," I said. "You're Effie Framingham."

The woman glanced about wildly, like she was worried someone would hear. After she realized no one was looking in our direction, she scowled.

She sniffed. "You are a pest."

"I have some questions," I said.

Effie Framingham glared. "Oh, *do* you? Well, here's

my answer: if you don't leave me alone, I'm going to call security."

Davey's hands turned into fists. I felt a rush of tenderness. I was supposed to be the one protecting him, not the other way around.

I straightened up as tall as I could and glared right back at her. "We live on Pelican Island. We found your statue in the marsh."

The old woman's eyes widened in surprise. I held my breath. Maybe she would tell us to go away. Maybe she'd hidden so many statues that she wouldn't know what I was talking about.

"Fine," she said. "Sit down."

I pulled up a chair, the heavy iron scraping on the brick patio. Davey perched at the edge of his, hugging his red backpack to his chest. I wished that I had something to hold on to.

Emotions flickered across Effie's face. She straightened the sketch pad in front of her. She pulled on the edge of her cape. She adjusted the silver clasp.

If it hadn't been for Davey, I might have rushed to ask a question. Because I was his sister, I knew the importance of waiting. Sometimes listening is the very best thing to do.

Finally, she seemed to shake herself out of her thoughts. When she looked up again, her eyes narrowed. "But how? It's deep underwater, on the remote side of the island. How could a child ever find it?"

My heart started beating fast. It really was her—this proved it. Davey's eyes were round. "Go on," he seemed to say. "You have to do this for both of us."

"It's because of the drought," I explained. "The water level is lower than it ever has been before."

Effie seemed to think this over. Finally, she sighed. "I never thought it would be found."

The corners of Effie's mouth curved in what could only be described as a smile. To be honest, her expression was still kind of scary—like she was setting a trap I was about to fall into. But there was a sparkle in her eyes. It gave me the confidence to go on.

I cleared my throat. "We're here to talk about the statue. Unless we can change the plan, a bridge is going to be built right where the statue is."

She tilted her side to the side. "What does this have to do with me?"

I paused, glancing at Davey.

"You don't understand," I said slowly. "The statue will be destroyed."

Effie sniffed. "That's progress, I guess."

My throat was suddenly dry. "Don't you *care*?"

Effie shrugged. "After I placed the sculpture, I let go of what would happen to it. I don't have a connection to it anymore."

Her words said one thing, but her face said another. I peered at her, trying to understand. "But you *do* care—I can tell."

Effie waved a wrinkled hand like she could wipe away my words.

I leaned forward in my seat. "Tell the county that the bridge will destroy your statue. Maybe they'll stop the project. It's obvious that a lot of people care about your art," I said. I refrained from saying that I personally didn't see what the fuss was about.

She let out a one-syllable laugh. "I wouldn't call a small exhibit in the Port Rogers art museum especially noteworthy."

I needed to convince her to try.

"The museum would help, too—I'm sure of it. When I wrote to them about the statue, they definitely wanted to know more. Even if the bridge can't be stopped, the museum could get the statue and keep it safe."

She snorted. "Way too heavy. Too complicated."

I didn't understand why she was pretending not to care. This wasn't a bunch of seashells and twigs. This was an actual statue, a real piece of art with its own shape and weight.

"Why wouldn't you save the statue if you could? I'm sure the museum would put it on display along with the other . . . art," I finished.

Effie glowered at me. "Weren't you paying attention to anything in there? That's not the art I'm interested in. I *used* to make statues like you found in the marsh. People bought them—kept them in museums or locked up behind glass. That's not what I do anymore."

I frowned. "But why?"

"Didn't you see the name of the exhibit?" Effie asked. "Ephemeral. Impermanent. Fleeting."

I folded my arms in front of me. As much as I enjoyed words, I didn't appreciate Effie Framingham acting like a walking thesaurus.

"I know the word means *temporary*," I said. "But why bother making art just for it to be destroyed?"

"You can't possibly understand," Effie said. "Your generation is digital *this* and computerized *that*. With a click-click-click, you can search up 'Renaissance art' and view it all on a pocket-size screen. But that's not what art is supposed to be. It's to be felt, to be seen, to be *smelled*. It's not a thing you can own and copy and print and make into one of those godforsaken photos with the words on them; what are they called?"

I paused, searching my brain. "Memes?" I finally asked.

"Memes," Effie repeated, nodding. "They're atrocious. My art is not meant to be captured. It is of the earth and to be acted on by the earth."

I looked at Davey, the genius, for help—but he seemed as lost as I was.

Effie gathered her cape around her shoulders. "It is the nature of creation that things will be lost. When I released that statue into the world, it stopped being mine. It's not yours, either, by the way. It belongs to the earth. Eventually, it will break down and become part of the universe again. If the bridge speeds up the process, then so be it."

My cheeks flamed. "How can you be okay with having something special and then losing it forever?"

Effie leaned back in her chair. "I made peace with that idea long ago."

My heart pounded in my chest. "I don't think you understand—"

Effie's eyes shone fiercely. "What makes you think *I* don't understand? I've lived a lot longer than you. I'm closer to dying than you are. I'm going to be dust again soon—all my carbon and hydrogen will be extracted and go back into the universe. Nothing lasts forever. Death and life are two sides of the same coin."

My throat squeezed. I didn't like thinking about death or dying. Not about characters in books. Not about animals on the side of the road or when I worried over Fritz in the salt marsh. It was certainly not a topic I wanted to discuss with this hateful person.

"Stop it," I said, my voice shaking.

Effie smirked. "I won't be less of who I am, even after I'm dead."

The day was hot, but I began to shiver. This conversation wasn't turning out like I'd hoped. I reached out my hand to touch the side of Davey's chair, trying to gather strength from him.

"But we've come all this way," I said, my voice pleading. "This means so much to us."

Effie was silent for a long moment. Her eyes narrowed.

"You keep saying the same thing," she said. "This statue is so important to us. We found it together in the marsh."

I didn't care about being polite anymore. "Yeah? So?"

"*So*," she said. "What do you mean, *we*?"

CHAPTER 25

I'm sorry.

I never meant to trick you, but I did. There's something I've been leaving out this whole time.

This story was a mystery. This story was an adventure. This story was about summer and siblings and a statue left in marsh mud.

But. There was another kind of story happening this whole time.

A sad story. A *crying* kind of story. One I never wanted to write.

(I hate sad stories.)

Let me back up and start again.

CHAPTER 26

The words hung in the air, heavy and full.

What did I mean, *we*?

I swiveled my head sideways.

But I didn't just *look*. I saw.

There were other people in the garden—the person with the baby, the men with name tags, and Effie Framingham herself, of course. But Davey wasn't in the chair next to me. It was only the red backpack. The one that used to belong to him.

I was alone, as I had been the entire summer.

I swallowed hard. There I sat, across from Effie Framingham. She looked like she didn't know what was about to happen. To be honest, I didn't know myself. But I could tell that it was time to say those words I'd been hiding from for so long—the real truth of what happened last summer.

It was the day I went to Millie's alone. The day he and I argued terribly. The day he decided to take his bike out on Sea Salt Boulevard, which was much too big and much too dangerous for a skinny nine-year-old. It was the day I knew I would feel alone forever. A heron without a stream. A breeze without a place to land. An Opal without her Fritz.

Last summer, Davey got hit by a car.

Last summer, Davey died instantly.

CHAPTER 27

I'm really, *really* sorry.

I know that a good writer tells the truth. And I'm trying so hard to be good.

But what is a writer with words that are all dried up? What is a sister without her brother?

I just wanted one more summer with him—one last adventure.

Also? I wanted you to know him. To maybe even love him a little. Because if I started the story after he was already dead, I knew you wouldn't see him in the same way—the skinny shoulders and mosquito bites, the potato-chip sandwiches and lopsided smile. You'd miss out on the way he swung his sneakers when sitting in the live oak high above the water. These are the things I needed you to know.

I didn't set out to lie to you, but I did. I can't take it back—the toothpaste is out of the tube. But I hope you will forgive me. Even though my heart is broken, I shouldn't have been reckless with yours.

I promise to tell you the real truth from now on. This is it:

On the day Davey died, my parents thought he was at Millie's with me. By the time they realized he was missing, the sun was setting and they were frantic. Our boats were accounted for, so we knew he wasn't in the marsh. But his bike—the ten-speed with a shiny bell, the same color of his favorite backpack—was gone.

An awful sound echoed in my mind. *You should learn to entertain yourself for once, Davey!*

If you loved me, you'd let me come along, he'd shouted. *You're a terrible sister.*

Those couldn't be the last words I'd ever say to him— the last words I'd ever hear back.

I waited at the window, staring at the empty driveway. Dad had taken his truck to look for Davey. Mrs. Ochoa and Millie were out searching for him, too. Mom paced, phone pressed to her ear. She dialed everyone she could think of—Mr. Harris at the visitors' center, the ferryboat crew, the police, all our neighbors and friends.

The view from our home had always given me peace, with trees framing the dock and that wide expanse of marsh. But I would have traded it all, forever, if it meant I could hear Davey ringing the bicycle bell, see him pumping his legs as hard as he could to bring himself home.

Instead, it was a black-and-white car that swung into view, gravel crunching beneath its tires. The sheriff got out and he was holding Davey's backpack. I froze. For the whole time he walked up to our porch, I was the only one in our family who knew.

When Mom heard a sound at the door, she spun to look—a mixture of hope and relief on her face. When she saw the backpack, she sank to her knees. Her cry was shattering. I felt it in my bones, like the earth was about to swallow us up.

My entire life, whenever something happened—little or big—I always looked to Davey. That's how we were. Always turning toward each other, always ready with a grin or a silly face. One look that said, "Can you believe that?" and another that replied, "Yes, I saw it, too."

The moment when Mom cried out, I automatically glanced around for Davey. A sharp pinch in my stomach told me that he wasn't there—that he wouldn't ever be there again. In that moment, my heart splintered into a thousand tiny shards. I squeezed my eyes shut.

But the moment I did, Davey's face appeared. I knew the specific way his eyebrows would draw together, and how his dark eyelashes would tremble, and the way he'd probably run right over to Mom and bury his head against her.

I had Davey memorized. I knew him by heart.

That's when I knew I'd never have to let him go—not really.

All I had to do was arrange my life so things made sense. Davey had never been much of a talker. It was easy to imagine that something could have happened that made his words disappear, except when we were alone together. Besides, I did hear him better when I was out at The Thumb, close to the marsh and the birds and the fish and the trees. When I was right next to everything he loved best.

I quit reading the newspaper so I wouldn't see anything about the accident. I stopped spending time with friends. It was much harder to imagine Davey clearly when others were around.

I pushed away Millie. If I hadn't gone to her house that day, Davey would still be alive. I should have kept him safe.

Being with Davey was the most important thing in my life. I knew how to hold on to him. I wouldn't let him go.

CHAPTER 28

One more thing, before getting back to Effie in the garden:

After the funeral—when the visitors had left a refrigerator full of casseroles—the house got quiet. My sadness had an unmistakable shape and weight. It reminded me of the times I'd forgotten a coaster on our oak coffee table. When I pulled away my water glass, a wet ring remained. That's what it was like. He was gone, but I could see and feel the exact place where he had been.

When Dad, Mom, and I were home at the same time, we drifted to separate corners of the house. It hurt to be apart, but it hurt just as much to be together. Our family had been four, and when we lost Davey, we were minus one. But somehow it was easier to be 1, 1, 1 instead of the number 3.

My brain was full of what-ifs. What if I'd never gone to Millie's that day. What if Davey had never learned to ride a bike in the first place. What if we still got to grow up together, like we were supposed to.

From the second I glimpsed the statue, I knew Davey would have loved it as much as I did. We needed one more adventure together. For one more summer, I would keep living in what-ifs.

CHAPTER 29

Effie was looking at me, and she was frowning.

"What is it, child?" she snapped. "You're sitting there, gaping like a fish."

"My brother," I said finally.

She gazed around the garden. "Where?"

I squeezed the red backpack to my chest. My face flushed. I thought I might get sick right there.

This is the thing about an island: news travels fast. Everyone heard about Davey without me having to tell them. I'd never actually spoken the words.

My mouth moved but no sounds came out. I swallowed hard and tried again.

"He died last summer," I said. "Davey. That's who I meant when I said *we.*"

Effie fixed me with a long look. Then she nodded

crisply. "You've lost someone. Usually I can tell when someone's had a great loss, but I missed it with you." Her voice sounded different than before. Not warm, exactly, but not quite so harsh.

I finally managed a nod.

She raised her eyebrow. "What's your name, anyway?"

"Bex," I squeaked. "Bex Wheeler."

She flipped the sketch pad open and rotated it toward me. "All right, Bex Wheeler. This is what you wanted to see, isn't it?"

On the page, Effie had drawn a little girl. Her cheeks were round and her hair gathered with a ribbon. Her dress fell in soft folds. I knew Effie Framingham was an artist—after all, I'd seen a whole show of her work. But this drawing was something else. Effie had put a whole person onto the page—one with hopes and fears, joys and sadness. From looking at the girl, I felt like I knew her.

"Are you an artist?" Effie asked.

I shook my head. "I can't draw."

Effie scoffed. "Art isn't necessarily *drawing*. It's about making something that wasn't there before."

I thought about the composition book in my backpack, the heavily erased page. "I used to write stories. I've been stuck for a while, though."

Effie shook her head. "A *writer*—I should have guessed. You look the type. Stubborn and sensitive, am I correct?"

Her bright eyes were sharp and probing. I had the

prickly sensation of meeting someone with X-ray vision, who could see through all my layers.

"Never feel bad about either one," she continued. "Artists have to be sensitive so they can feel deeply. They have to be stubborn to develop a point of view."

"I guess I am those things," I admitted. "Sometimes."

She leaned back, a satisfied smile on her face.

I looked at the drawing again. It had a gentleness I hadn't noticed in the work from the exhibit.

"Who is she?"

Effie's gaze lingered on the page for a moment before answering. "My daughter, Abigail. You aren't the only one to love someone and lose them."

She said the last words so quietly, I thought I'd imagined them. From the look on her face, though, I knew I hadn't.

"What happened?" I asked.

"Cancer," she said, spitting the word out like it left a bitter taste in her mouth. "Yours?"

"Car accident."

"At least it was quick," she said. "You probably didn't have to see him in pain. Not so for Abigail."

I hated it when people said *at least* this or *at least* that. Like I'm supposed to feel grateful about it.

"At least *you* got to say goodbye," I said. "At least *you* never had to blame yourself."

Effie pointed a long finger at her chest. "Who says I didn't?"

My eyes widened. "You feel like it's your fault?"

"For a long time, I did," she said. "Do *you*?"

I nodded. "He shouldn't have taken his bike on that road. If I'd been with him, it never would have happened."

Effie lowered her hand. "You don't know that."

"I was the oldest," I whispered. "I would have stopped him."

Effie shrugged elaborately. "Who's to say? Maybe he'd have argued. Maybe you'd have followed. Maybe your parents would have buried two and not one."

I felt dizzy, like I was standing up high, teetering on an edge. Usually, when something about Davey came up, people gave me sad eyes that said, "Poor Bex." No one talked about him dying. No one tried to make me think about it in a different way.

"Be careful with the blaming," Effie continued. "Sometimes holding on to that pain is a way to try to keep them here with us. I sometimes slide into those thoughts myself. Abigail had a cough for a while and I kept putting off taking her to the doctor, one thing or another. She bruised easily. I thought she was tender-skinned."

I thought of my what-ifs—the way I'd go over them again and again when it was late at night. When I wished so hard to have him back.

"But really, those thoughts are a way of keeping them *from* us. Those thoughts are ugliness. I'd rather hold on to the lovely parts. The way her eyelids fluttered as she dreamed. The way she splashed in rain puddles. The way she loved the sea. Those are the only things I wish to keep," Effie said.

I was quiet for a moment. So much of Effie's art had to do with letting go. Was that because of Abigail?

I leaned forward. "Is that why your art changed from sculptures to—"

I caught myself. I'd almost said that her new works were "the weird stuff," but I was pretty sure that would have insulted her. And I wanted her to keep talking.

Luckily, she didn't notice. Her gaze softened, like she was remembering something from a long time ago.

"After she died, I didn't make art for a long time," she said. "I was too hollow. Do you know what I mean by that?"

I looked at her, startled. That was the perfect word. I couldn't put words on a page when I felt so empty inside. I was afraid to be reckless with my own tender heart.

Effie tucked a curl behind her ear. "Eventually, I realized that art is a part of who I am. I had to do it again to build myself up. I couldn't give in to despair."

I turned over her words in my mind. She talked about creating like it was easy to do. It wasn't like that for me and writing—my words refused to come.

The corner of Effie's mouth quirked up in a wistful way. "That statue you found was one of my first projects after she died. I wanted to make something beautiful and look at it every day. But after a while, I decided to place it somewhere secret. The day I left it in the marsh was an exquisite kind of torture. Driving away, I was out of my mind. But eventually, I felt peace. She was one with the universe again. I had to let her go."

Irritation sparked inside me. If Effie *really* cared about her art, she wouldn't leave it out there to rot away in the marsh.

"For a long time, I did other projects—things that wouldn't last," Effie continued. "I didn't want anything that could be bought or sold. I didn't want to make anything that could be *owned*."

She tapped her fingertips together, like she had finished making her point. I thought of her circles in the sand, the waves that washed away the patterns. As I did, I began to feel more confused than ever.

"Why do you hide?" I asked. "The museum said your whereabouts were unknown. They didn't even know if you were still alive."

Effie sniffed. "I used to crave recognition. It used to make me feel like I had arrived. But now I know that fire comes from within. I make art because that is who I am. I don't need museums anymore."

"But you came anyway," I said.

She arched an eyebrow. "I'm only human. And they did a nice job, when all is said and done."

I was so busy thinking about what to ask next that I barely noticed the activity on the far side of the garden.

"There she is; there she is!"

I turned my head to see what the commotion was. Running toward me, followed closely by a team of security guards, were my parents. And they did not look happy.

CHAPTER 30

Before I could say a word, Mom and Dad pulled me to my feet. They hugged me so hard, I thought my ribs might stick together permanently.

"Where have you been—"

"We were so afraid—"

"Of all the things to do, Bex—"

"So glad you're safe—"

"All the way to Port Rogers, what were you ever thinking?"

They were the kinds of questions that didn't need answering, at least not in that moment.

My cheeks were wet and someone was wailing—and then I realized that it was me. I was *sobbing*, and they were crying, too. Although I guessed I was in big trouble, I was really glad to see them.

The security guards' radios squawked and they notified the others that I had been found. I looked for Effie, but she must have slipped away in the shuffle.

We went to the dock and waited for the next ferryboat. Mom and Dad stood on either side of me, like they thought I'd bolt away if given the chance.

"How did you find me?" I asked.

"Millie," Mom answered simply.

Millie! My hands clenched. I couldn't believe she'd betrayed me.

Dad raised his eyebrow. "Wipe that look off your face, Bex. Mom found your boat without you in it and she was frantic."

Mom's smile wobbled like she was about to start weeping.

"I'm so sorry," I said. "I didn't think you'd know I was gone."

"Of course we noticed," Mom said. "You've wanted independence, but we've been keeping an eye on you. Other people have been, too."

I thought of Mr. Harris then and his rumbly voice telling me I'd be okay. Mrs. Ochoa always with a hug or a treat from the store. Even Mary Ellen and the extra-buttery popcorn. Sometimes the heart sees what it wants, but sometimes it misses what's been there the entire time.

I looked back and forth at them. Mom's glasses were tear-splotched. Dad somehow seemed smaller than usual.

I'd been so wrapped up in myself and the statue, I hadn't thought about how they might feel if they realized I was gone.

"Am I in trouble?" I asked.

"You scared a lot of people, including Mom and me," Dad said slowly. "I want you to know that—but you're not in trouble. Not exactly."

Mom reached over and brushed my hair out of my eyes. "Mostly, we want to understand. I think we need to have a talk."

"It's been long overdue," Dad agreed.

My eyelids felt heavy. I tried to nod, but it only made me realize how tired I was.

On the ferry, we picked a bench in a tucked-away corner. Dad wrapped one arm around me. Mom's cool fingers traced a figure-eight pattern on my forehead. The whole time, I clutched Davey's backpack to my chest. The salt air and the steady motion of the ferryboat calmed me. A few of the crew looked at us curiously but no one interrupted. It was like they could tell we needed to be in a bubble, just the three of us.

Water and land passed by until we finally disembarked. We walked home the long way, past the familiar houses and porches and gardens. It was the first time all year that I'd been with my parents without imagining Davey's reaction to everything. I felt turned around and upside down, like I'd lost my place on the map. But it was also good to be with them like that. Mom reached over to squeeze my hand and I squeezed back.

My breath caught in my throat when I saw our house. It seemed as if days and weeks had passed since this morning. We went inside. Squish meowed a hello, butting her head against my shins until I picked her up. I'd been picturing her with Davey all summer, but I had to admit that she'd been checking in with me this whole time.

I buried my face in her soft fur. She might not love me the same way she loved my brother, but she was a better cat than I gave her credit for.

Mom made three mugs of mint tea and we sat on the sofa together. It was like they needed me close—even Squish curled heavy in my lap.

Dad cleared his throat. "It's been pretty clear that you've been up to something lately. Mom thought we should take you to therapy, but I wanted to give you space. I regret that."

Mom folded her legs under her. "We were under the impression that you've been spending lots of time with Millie. But that isn't the case, is it?"

They waited for me to talk. My chest ached, like I had swallowed something sharp.

"I haven't done anything with Millie since the day Davey died," I said.

Dad's eyebrows popped up. He rubbed the top of his head, making his red hair stick up straight.

Mom frowned like she was trying to understand. "But why? She's one of your oldest friends."

I took a deep breath. At first, the words came in a trickle. But as I gained momentum, they came out in a rush.

How I blamed Millie for Davey getting hit by the car.

How I blamed myself.

How I'd been imagining Davey with me every step of the way.

The way we found the statue and why we went to Port Rogers.

The fact that the new bridge meant I might lose the place where I was closest to him.

I told them the whole story. When I finished, Dad sighed.

"I hate the idea of you spending so much time alone—I wish we'd known," he said.

I stared down at my lap. "But I *wasn't* alone—at least, I never felt that way. It was like he was with me the whole time. It meant I didn't have to let him go."

Mom squeezed my hand. "He'll always be with you, Bex."

I shook my head. "But I don't want him in my imagination. I want him here—really here."

"Me too," Dad said, placing his mug on the coffee table. "That's probably part of why I've been picking up so many extra shifts. I feel close to Davey when I'm looking out at the water. I write poems for him sometimes, in my head."

When he said the last part, the tips of his ears flamed red. I had no idea that Dad had a place where he felt extra connected to Davey, too.

Mom scratched Squish under the chin. "I feel that way about Davey's room—it's like a peace comes over me when I'm there, surrounded by his things."

I remembered the day I'd found her there, asleep. Finding Davey's things in a box upset me. But I'd never stopped to wonder why Mom had been there in the first place.

Until that moment, Dad, Mom, and I had been separate in our sadness. But it was beginning to dawn on me that they were the only people in the world who had a chance of understanding what I was feeling—not in a general way, like Effie Framingham had. But in the specific way of missing Davey. Like me, they knew the exact shape and weight of losing one freckle-faced, skinny-shouldered, nose-in-a-book nine-year-old boy.

A warmth surged in my chest. I set down my mug with a *thunk*. "I want to take you to The Thumb. Right now."

My insides jumped around like they were about to bubble over. I had to show them the place that was so important to Davey and me.

Mom's brow furrowed. "It's getting late. Tomorrow?"

"I've got an early shift," Dad said.

A wave of sadness washed over me. If Dad had to work, it would probably get pushed off again and again until we'd drifted back to our corners. The bridge would be built, the statue smashed, and The Thumb would be gone. There was never a guarantee about what would last. I wanted them to see it as soon as possible, before it changed forever.

Tears stung my eyes. I wanted to close my eyes to block them. It would be easier to let my thoughts slide sideways to Davey. What his face would look like. How he'd mutter, "Parents! They just don't get it."

Squish turned her face to me. Her eyes were bright green, like sunshine on cordgrass. She blinked her eyes once, slowly.

I paused. It couldn't be—could it?

Then she did it again. "I love you," she was saying.

I'll never be a cat expert—not like Davey—but I got the message. Love is how a family holds together. I had to try again.

"Dad," I said, my voice scratching. "This is important. *Please can we go? Tomorrow?*"

Dad rubbed the top of his head. "I'll figure it out, Bex-Bean."

Mom covered a yawn. "This has been a very long day."

Dad stretched, patting his belly. "Any ideas for food?"

"I know what to do," I said. They exchanged glances over my head but didn't ask. I went to the kitchen and made our supper.

I returned carrying three plates: each with slices of toasted oatmeal bread, spread with a thick layer of almond butter and a thin layer of raspberry jam, topped with half a banana and sprinkled with a dusting of potato chips.

Mom grinned. "Davey sandwiches."

Dad took a big bite. "Mmm—these are excellent! How come we never tried them before?"

"I thought they would taste strange," Mom admitted. "But somehow, it works."

I smiled to myself and chewed my sandwich. It was sweet and salty, crunchy and smooth, with a trace of bitterness. It had everything at once.

CHAPTER 31

The next morning when I came downstairs, Mom and Dad waited at the kitchen table.

Mom's face brightened. She stood up and gave me a big hug. "Good morning, sweetheart. Ready for breakfast?"

I nodded. She stacked piping hot pancakes on my plate and drizzled boysenberry syrup on top. I sat down beside Dad and dug in.

He swallowed a drink of coffee. "As soon as you're finished, we'll head out to The Thumb. Elijah Harris said he'd be happy to take my shift."

Good old Mr. Harris. If he were here, I could have hugged him. But since he wasn't, I decided to hug Dad.

"Easy there," he said, patting my back.

After breakfast, we walked outside together. When I

saw the dock, I gasped. The family canoe was in the water, but my rowboat was missing.

"The *True Blue*—where is it?" Then I remembered. "I left it on the shore by the park yesterday morning."

"It will be fine, Bex," Mom said. "We'll get it later."

We hadn't been in the canoe since Davey died. His seat was empty, of course. Squish sniffed the air briefly and then came to sit by me.

Dad pushed off and we began our journey to The Thumb. The sky was overcast and the water still. Dragonflies darted past, zipping through the cordgrass, and fiddler crabs waved their claws from the shore.

In the canoe, we looked in just one direction: ahead. It seemed like a small difference—but for me, it changed everything. I'd traveled through those streams since I was old enough to curl my fingers around an oar, but on that day, it was like I was seeing the marsh for the first time. Maybe it was a trick of the light. Maybe it was viewing things from a different angle. Or maybe it was the fact that I could see where we were going instead of looking at where we'd been.

Every so often, Dad asked me to direct him. I had to pause for a moment to get my bearings. Little by little, I got us where we needed to go.

When we arrived at The Thumb, Dad hopped out, pushing the canoe all the way up onto the sand. I carried Squish to dry ground. Immediately, she began investigating an empty mussel shell.

I pointed at branches. "This is where I always sat. That was Davey's favorite spot."

Dad traced his fingers on the trunk's spray-painted orange "X." Mom wanted to know the exact spot where Davey had read his favorite books.

When Dad asked about the dried-out cordgrass in the water, I told him about the River Sticks.

Then I showed them the rocky side of the peninsula and explained how I'd met the builders that day.

I saved the statue for last. Together, the three of us waded in the water. Mom and Dad examined it carefully, exclaiming about how unusual it was. They listened when I told them how I'd met Effie Framingham and her thoughts about holding on and letting go.

"Such a shame for it to be stuck out here where no one can see it," Dad said.

I knew what he meant. But for Effie, the fact the statue existed was enough. She hated the idea of it being locked up.

Mom peered at the water. "So many crabs—I've never seen so many in one place."

Dad and I smiled at each other. Leave it to Mom to find a way to think about the ecosystem.

After a while, we went back to the shore. Mom handed me a soft towel.

Dad stretched his arms over his head. "This is a special place. Thanks for bringing us."

Mom rubbed my back. "I liked hearing your Davey stories."

"I liked talking about him," I said quietly. For some reason, I was feeling shy.

"Do you want to know one of my favorite memories?" Dad asked. "He was only four or five—a tiny thing—and the two of us went to breakfast at the diner in Port Rogers. He studied that menu for what seemed like ages, and then he finally decided he would have the Pirate's Plate, which came with two eggs, any style. When they asked how to make them, he said that he'd have them deviled."

I knew what deviled eggs were. Mrs. Ochoa made really good ones, hard cooked to perfection and topped with lots of smoked paprika. She always used Duke's Mayonnaise because it was the best.

"But that means scrambled or over easy," I said. "Not *deviled*."

Dad nodded. "The server grinned and said they'd see what they could do. Wouldn't you know that the chef himself brought out a plate of hash browns, sausage, and two perfect deviled eggs on the side. Said he hoped they were up to Davey's standards."

We all cracked up. I guess Davey knew more than the rest of us sometimes.

Mom straightened her glasses. "Once I found him staring at the water, slowly opening and closing his eyes. When I asked him about it, he said he was taking pictures with the camera in his brain."

A warmth spread inside me. I wrapped up tightly in

the towel, smiling and thinking of all the good things about Davey. We sat on the shore for hours, sharing memories. Sometimes we talked and sometimes we were quiet. Sometimes we laughed and talked and other times we cried and hugged. It was sad and happy, mixed up together.

I unzipped the red backpack and gave them each a yellow M&M. I explained that I always took my time with them because I never knew when Davey would give me another. I was letting the sweetness melt across my tongue just as sure as sunshine when I heard a low rumble.

All three of us turned our faces upward.

Plink.

Plink.

Plonk!

First one drop. Then another. Then more. Until the sound surrounded us, pattering on the tree leaves, plinking on the canoe, ker-plunking in the water.

"Rain!" I gasped.

"Mercy!" Mom grinned at the sky. "Thank goodness."

Dad removed his cap and the rain splatted on his head.

Squish hissed, pressing herself against the tree trunk. She seemed confused—maybe, after all this time without rain, she'd forgotten what it was.

"Grab her," Dad advised. "We don't want her climbing to a branch we can't reach."

I scooped her up and we stood under the tree.

Mom looked at the clouds. "Do you think it will clear up?"

Dad shook his head. "This one's been a long time coming."

"But . . . the statue! Will it get covered by the water?" I asked.

Mom patted my shoulder. They didn't answer.

I could almost see the water rising as rain poured down. I held Squish to my chest, her tiny heartbeat pounding against my fingers.

Dad grabbed the life jackets out of the canoe and tossed them to Mom and me. "We better get going."

I wrapped Squish in my sweatshirt. She wiggled to get away.

"No, Squish," I said firmly. "This is for your own good. Otherwise you might get a chill."

We got in the canoe together. Both Mom and Dad paddled with fluid strokes and I held Squish tight. When we were halfway home, a bolt of jagged lightning streaked across the sky.

"Faster," Dad said. Rain was one thing, but lightning was dangerous, especially out on the water.

When we returned to shore, Dad pushed the canoe in. "Go inside," he said.

I hesitated. "The *True Blue*. We have to go get it."

Mom shook her head. "It's not safe. The ground is too dry to absorb all this rain, so there's a chance of flash flooding. Hurry inside, Bex—we'll be right behind you."

I ran across the yard and went through the back door. My sweatshirt had mostly protected Squish, but she was a little damp. Miraculously, she allowed me to dry her before she wiggled away.

Mom and Dad came inside in time to see her swishing upstairs, head held high.

Dad laughed. "It seems that being caught in the storm insulted her dignity."

The sky had darkened. The rain fell in sheets, thick and fast. A wide puddle began to form in the flat spot in the yard.

"We should get into dry clothes," Mom said.

I went upstairs, but then something made me stop fast. Squish was curled on my bed—she'd picked *my* room, not Davey's.

I shut the door behind me. "Wow. Really?"

Squish fixed me with her green stare.

I eased myself onto the mattress. Squish watched me with narrowed eyes. Slowly, I moved my hand toward her until I was petting her back. Eventually, she relaxed.

"There," I whispered. "That's not so bad, is it?"

Then she started to purr—a buzzy sound that rumbled from her throat to my fingertips. It was almost as if I could feel the vibrations all the way in my heart. I forgot about my wet clothes. Thunder crashed outside, but inside we were cozy and warm.

CHAPTER 32

It poured for three days.

When the skies finally cleared, everything seemed greener. The grass was springier. The flowers were brighter. Even the trees stood straighter.

Mom shook her head. "We needed that. Look how high the water level is."

On our dock, the water reached higher than it had in months. Water crept across the sandy edge of our yard.

"The *True Blue*," I said.

"I'll go with you," Mom said.

Together we took the road to Mooney Park. The rain had swept blossoms from the crepe myrtle trees, so it looked like the sidewalks were covered with colorful bursts of confetti.

We walked through the park's flat playground area and then carefully climbed down the steep hill to the marsh.

"I used to push you for hours on that tire swing," Mom said.

Usually, when I thought of Davey, my chest squeezed tight. I waited, but that feeling didn't come. Instead, I had a mix of feelings. Sad that Davey wasn't there with us. But also happy, picturing the times we'd played here together.

"Remember how he liked to lean backward while he was swinging?" I asked.

Mom gave me a happy-sad smile. "He said he wanted to watch the sky, but it made him so dizzy."

"He always said it was worth it," I reminded her.

As we headed down the incline, something looked strange. The hill was different—shorter than it had been before.

Mom whistled low. "It flooded."

I scanned the area, looking but not fully processing what I saw.

"There!" Mom said, pointing.

A few branches and leaves rose up from the water's surface.

My eyes widened. "The bushes are underwater? But that means my boat is *gone*?"

Mom shook her head slowly. "I've never seen anything like it. The water level must have risen enough to carry it away."

I clenched my fists. Tears sprang in my eyes. It wasn't fair. That boat was everything to me—and to Davey, too. Years of memories washed over me.

"I think I'm going to be sick," I said. A lump formed in my throat.

"We'll find it," Mom said. "It's probably in the marsh somewhere, lodged against a sandbar."

But Mom was wrong. We looked everywhere for that boat, but it didn't turn up. The *True Blue* was gone.

PART FIVE

CHAPTER 33

In its own quiet way, summer began turning to fall.

The days no longer blurred into one another. There was a flurry of last-minute appointments for doctor and dentist checkups, which Dad said were easier to schedule during vacation. Then there was my school's cheerful notice regarding seventh-grade orientation. A bundle of sweaters and leggings that appeared, washed and folded, on my bedspread along with Mom's note suggesting that I sort my warm-weather clothes into Keep or Donate piles.

But there was a day coming that didn't need a postcard reminder or email confirmation. Even if I never peeked at a calendar, I still would have known. The signs were impossible to miss—the sun's angle in the sky, the sudden urgency of squirrels, the whispers of crisp air around the edges of the day. It was almost the one-year anniversary of Davey's death. We'd had a whole year without him, and nature had her own summer clean-out project underway.

One afternoon, I sat outside under the big magnolia, looking at the water. The day of the museum adventure seemed like it happened ages ago. We never did find the *True Blue*, which was a tender spot for me. I hated being stuck on land. It made me feel trapped.

Sometimes I accompanied Mom on the kayak to do her research. She'd taken an interest in the area around the statue, so we made several trips to The Thumb. Mostly she sampled water and soil, the data filling neat rows in her weatherproof notebook. Meanwhile, I borrowed Davey's idea of a brain camera and tried to memorize that part of the marsh, which was about to change forever. Sometimes we saw scattered stakes and markings—evidence that the developers had been there. I had a nightmare where the live oak was talking to me, angry that I hadn't done more. It made me want to cry every time I thought about it.

Mom, Dad, and I spent evenings on the screened porch playing cards, listening to music, and telling stories. Davey was always on our minds. For a long time, this was what had kept us apart. But, eventually, he became the thing that brought us back together.

I looked down at my black composition book. The page was blank. I was as stuck as always.

"Hey," said a voice.

I glanced up. It was Millie, lowering herself onto the grass next to me. "My grandma told me about everything. Are you okay?"

I pushed my bangs out of my eyes. "Sometimes yes, sometimes no."

Millie nodded. "The feelings are all over the place, right? That's what my dad said after my grandma died."

I squinted, not sure what she meant. I knew for a fact that Mrs. Ochoa was strong and healthy. I'd seen her on her electric scooter earlier that day. "Your grandma?"

Millie fiddled with one of her gold earrings. "My *other* grandma. She died in January."

"Oh," I said. "I didn't know."

Millie hesitated. Too late, I remembered her letters stuffed in my desk drawer. Maybe she had tried to tell me, but I didn't listen.

"These were hers," she said, pointing at her ears. Earlier in the summer, I'd thought her jewelry meant she was acting fancy. Instead, she was trying to hold on to a memory of someone she loved. I could understand that.

"Anyway," Millie continued. "Some people say that it gets a little bit better every day, but it doesn't. Some days are better and some days are worse. Some days start out one way and end up another. After someone dies, feelings don't go in a straight line."

I thought about this for a while.

"Sometimes when I have a good day, I end up feeling bad about it," I said. "Guilty, even."

Millie wrinkled her forehead in thought. "Because you're worried that it's not fair to Davey?"

I nodded. "Also because when I'm sad, it's a way of keeping him close by."

We were quiet for a while. A heron flew past, flapping its wings and holding its legs straight out behind.

"I'm sorry about your grandma," I said finally. "And I'm sorry about this summer. It wasn't your fault. I felt awful about going to your house without Davey and I didn't want to be reminded of it."

Millie tilted her head. "Do you still feel that way?"

Mostly no, I wanted to tell her. *But sometimes yes.*

I shrugged. "He was my brother. We should have been able to grow up together."

Millie blew out a deep breath. "It's really, super, terribly unfair. It stinks."

"Davey knew everything about me and he loved me anyway," I said. "That's gone now."

"You're *still* his sister," Millie said quickly.

"I know," I said. "But it's like that version of me is lost."

We were quiet for a moment, looking at the water for a while.

Millie cleared her throat. "I know it isn't the same, but I've known you for a long time, Bex. And I knew Davey, too. If you need me to remind you of what it was like when we were all together, I can do that whenever you want."

An invisible knot loosened inside me. We looked at the water together for a while. And then we started talking—not about Davey. Not about anything in particular—the island and friends and her soccer tryouts. She taught me how to say "pimple" in Mandarin, Spanish, and French.

Mom came home on her kayak. When she saw that Millie and I were talking, she smiled and brought us lemonade in tall green glasses.

After we'd finished talking, Millie stood up.

"I need to pack," she said, smoothing her dress.

In some ways, it was sad that we hadn't spent any time together that summer. But it was good to know we were still friends.

"I'll write to you," I said.

A slow smile spread across her face. "I'd like that."

She started to head back to her grandma's but then stopped and spun around. "Bex? I'm sorry about your boat."

My shoulders sank. "Me too."

Millie bit her lip. "It's not in the marsh, so it must have washed out to the ocean, right? Maybe it's having some adventures out there on its own."

The image popped in my mind—the *True Blue*, sailing bravely over ocean waves.

"I like that idea," I said.

Millie grinned and turned again, walking with a bounce in her step. I thought back to the day at the museum. Effie had said that she could usually tell when someone had experienced a loss. My friends at school didn't talk about Davey. It was like entire topics had been erased from the vocabulary of our friendship: summers, cars, siblings. One time, Grace complained about her little brother sticking chewed-up bubble gum inside her sneakers. But when she realized what she was saying, her eyes got big and round and she clapped her hand over her mouth. I wanted to tell her it was okay. I wanted to tell her that I know that some people still have their brothers, and that all brothers are annoying sometimes. But I didn't know how to find those words.

It wasn't like that with Millie. Millie knew that I needed to remember him, even when it was sad. Millie had lost someone, too. It wasn't the same, but it was something. It reminded me of the socks Mom wanted me to donate—the ones with the stretched-out elastic. After a heart stretches out, it never goes back to the same shape. But maybe sometimes there's more room than there was before.

CHAPTER 34

When I went back inside, Mom was leaning against the kitchen counter. The table was set with cloth napkins and candles, and in the center was a large manila envelope.

"What's going on?" I asked.

Mom waved her hand. "I'll tell you after we sit down. Help me with these green beans, please."

I glanced at Dad, who shrugged. He didn't seem to know, either.

Finally, after all the dishes had been passed, Mom grinned wide. "The first time we went out to The Thumb, I was surprised by the number of crabs—blues and fiddlers. I started to wonder if the statue had something to do with it."

"Why would crabs care about a statue?" I asked.

"Bex," she said in her science-teacher voice. "Do you remember what the statue was made of?"

"Metal," I answered. "Greenish-colored."

"Copper—when it oxidizes, it turns green," Mom said. "It's a mineral that's essential for life. I wondered why the blue crabs were there—possibly, they wanted to eat the fiddler crabs. Then I wondered why the *fiddler* crabs were there. I started to take samples and found out that the copper levels were higher there around the statue."

I felt lost. Mom was always getting excited about some science thing or another, and it was starting to seem like one of those times.

Mom opened the envelope and slid out a stack of papers. "I examined my samples. Then I found something else."

She flipped through the pages, finally stopping at one and holding it up.

"It's a diatom—a type of algae," she said. "So small it can only be seen under a microscope."

Mom pushed the paper in my direction. It was a print-out of a photograph. The creature had a somewhat rectangular body with lines and dots inside. Long hairs flowed from each side.

"It looks like a miniature alien," I said.

Mom's smile widened. "I sent it to a lab to get its genome sequenced, so they could tell if it had already been identified."

I handed the page to Dad, who studied it carefully.

"And?" I asked.

"It's new," Mom said. "It's never been discovered before."

Dad beamed. "That's wonderful, honey. I'm so proud of you!"

I picked up the paper and studied the image. It was a funny-looking thing. "What did they decide to call it?"

"That's why I wanted to talk to you both," she said slowly. "When there's a new species, the person who discovers it gets to do the naming."

Dad and I exchanged looks.

"*You* get to name it?" I asked.

Mom took a deep breath. "The first part is *Chaetoceros*, which is the genus. The species would be *daveyia*. After Davey. If that's okay with both of you."

"Yes," I said quickly. Dad nodded.

"It's so small," Mom said. "But it's very important."

I rolled the words around in my mind. *Chaetoceros daveyia*. It had a good ring to it. Small but important. Just like Davey himself.

CHAPTER 35

The next day, my own letter came in the mail. The front of the envelope said *Bex Wheeler, Pelican Island.*

I tore it open.

Dear Bex,

It's me—the old lady you met at the museum. I didn't have your street address, but I thought the mail carrier would know where to deliver it.

The only reason I let you sit at my table was because you reminded me of my Abigail. I think about her each day and I suppose I always will. I expect it's the same with you and Davey.

This is what I was about to tell you before the hubbub started: you don't have to imagine your brother being with you. The simple truth? He is with you already. Davey is part of you, as my Abigail is part of me. When we do good things in the world, it's a way for them to live on.

So this is to say: you should stop thinking and set about <u>doing</u>. You said you write stories and that you've been stuck. The only way forward is to start, even if you don't know where you'll end up.

I'm taking my own advice. After all these years, I've started a new piece. It's about letting go, but it's also about holding on. Sometimes it's important to do both.

That's it for now. I'll keep you posted. You can feel free to send me your stories if you want.

CHAPTER 36

The one-year anniversary came. We decided to make it a day Davey would have enjoyed, if he were still alive. So we went to an arcade and got ice cream and watched a complicated movie about whales.

Just before supper, Dad asked me to help with a project in the shed. But when he opened the doors, I saw what was waiting inside: a two-person canoe, the exact color of a yellow M&M.

"Dad," I gasped. "I love it."

Dad grinned, pulling his ball cap low. "Are you sure? I know it's not the same as the rowboat."

I hugged him. "It's perfect. I can't wait to take it for a spin."

Dad glanced at his watch. "You probably have time."

He didn't have to say it twice. I ran inside to grab the

red backpack. By the time I came back out, Dad had carried the canoe to shore.

"Want company?" Dad asked.

I buckled my life jacket. "Another time. There's something I have to do by myself."

Dad waved as I paddled away.

The late afternoon was bright and the water seemed to glow. A heron stalked its prey, fiddler crabs waved from the sand, and a squadron of pelicans flew overhead.

When I got to The Thumb, I pushed my canoe onto the land. I dropped the red backpack at my feet and rummaged through it. Then I took out my black composition book, a pen, and a clear plastic jar filled to the top with yellow M&M's. I popped one in my mouth and let it melt across my tongue.

The wind blew from the east, sending a rush of air into the live oak. I closed my eyes, hearing the rustle of leaves. The marsh had its own music, and Davey had taught me to listen.

A familiar chittering sounded from across the marsh. I opened my eyes in time to glimpse two sleek and slippery creatures clambering into the water.

"Fritz and Opal," I breathed. I hadn't seen them since before the storm. But there they were, like always. Fritz's torn ear flapped as he hurried to catch up with his stronger, faster sister.

"You had me worried!" I called out. Of course they didn't answer—they were busy hunting for supper.

They swam and dove until they each pulled a crab onto the shore.

So much had happened in a short time. The construction was officially suspended. Thanks to Mom's discovery, studies had to be completed before the project could continue. At least for a while, The Thumb would stay as it was. Still, I knew the bridge might come someday.

I used to think that if I lost The Thumb, I'd also lose my brother. But that won't happen—not when I have the wind in my face and the smell of salt air in my nose. Not when I have the sure sunshine of a yellow M&M melting across my tongue. Sometimes it's the things you can't see that make the biggest difference.

When high tide comes in the marsh, there's a popping sound almost like a tongue clicking. It's from all the mussels opening to allow the water to rush into their shells. Just like me, they stick tight to the place they call home. Like me, they're ready for what happens next.

Telling the truth thoroughly, constantly, and recklessly isn't easy—but it is important. And it was time to start doing that again, no matter what.

I opened my composition book and uncapped my pen. Effie said I should start, even if I didn't know exactly where I was going.

Luckily, I knew where to begin: that moment when what we see and touch becomes what we feel and remember. The moment when sea becomes sky.

Acknowledgments

Marietta Zacker, it would be easy to focus on all the encouragement and every "yes" you've given me over the years—but this book only came about because you had the wisdom and strength to give me one very important *no.* Thank you for believing in me all those years ago when I said I didn't know how to fix it but I would someday.

Mary Kate Castellani, I can definitely say that I've never worked so hard on a project, and much of that is due to your insight and guidance. I'll always remember our first conversation about this book—before I'd even written a word!—and I appreciate the way you believed that I could do it.

Jackie Skahill, I came into your seventh-grade classroom still grieving, with so many stories inside me that didn't know where to go. I am thankful every day for you and the amount of writing I got to do in your class. You and Dan have always been in my corner, and I love you both to pieces.

Thank you to Andy and Jared Turner for being my brothers. Andy, you taught me so much in your nine years on Earth. I'll always miss you and your big, wonderful laugh. Jared, you teach me every day about being a good person. I'm so lucky to be a part of your life.

Aislinn Estes and Gauri Johnston, I could live a thousand lifetimes and never find better friends. I'm so lucky to have your brilliant minds, keen insight, shoulders to cry on, hilarious senses of humor, and gigantic hearts. Love you both.

Brigid Kemmerer, thank you for reading so many early pages and for holding my hand almost constantly throughout the process of writing this book. Your encouragement was priceless and so is your friendship.

Many friends supported me while I was writing—whether it was listening to plot details or reading pages or just being a wonderful part of my world. There are too many to include them all, but I'd like to give special thanks to Jasmine Warga, Mariama Lockington, Lisa Moore Ramée, Jess Redman, Laurie Morrison, Rajani LaRocca, Nicole Panteleakos, Jodi Picoult, Heather Clark, Josh Levy, Chris Baron, Wendy Chen, Jennifer Springer, Sam Flynn, Christina Haisty, Jen Shapiro, Jessica Kramer, Anna Totten, Ashley Bernier, Naomi Milliner, Cory Leonardo, Ginny and Ed McDunn, Pat and Bob Elliott, and Caroline Flory. Thanks and hugs to Mandy Roylance for our many talks over lunch about this story and life in general and to Mandy

Hemingway for being the kindest, most thoughtful, best care-package-delivering neighbor that anyone could ever ask for.

Thank you to the team at Bloomsbury, including: Erica Barmash, Faye Bi, Erica Chan, Nicholas Church, Phoebe Dyer, Beth Eller, Alona Fryman, Noella James, Lex Higbee, Donna Mark, Kathleen Morandini, Kei Nakatsuka, Oona Patrick, Laura Phillips, and Lily Yengle. Enormous thanks to Yaoyao Ma Van As and Jeanette Levy for making the most perfect art and design for the story. Thank you to everyone at Gallt & Zacker for all the support. Big thanks to all teachers, librarians, reviewers, podcasters, and booksellers who put my books into the hands of readers—I appreciate you so much! For early reads and support, thank you Beth Seufer Buss, Jamie Rogers Southern, Lupe Penn, Joy Preble, Hannah Oxley, Jen Kraar, Bridey Morris, Christina Batten, Abbe Townsend, Carol Moyer, Alyssa Raymond, and Rayna Nielsen. I hope to visit you all in your bookstores sometime in the near future!

And now, the part where my words could never be enough—my family.

I'm so thankful for my kind, brave, and beautiful children. Nora, I thank you for all the playlists and silly reels and homemade treats and your thoughtful, creative soul. Leo, I thank you for your unique way of seeing the world, for walks with Friday, for reminding me not to look when something scary or gross is on TV. Olive, you inspire me by being yourself—thank you for finding every loophole, for your sense of justice, and for making me laugh every day. Seeing the three of you together fills my heart with joy and I hope you'll always be there for each other. I love you backwards and forwards and upside-down.

Thank you to our dog, Friday, who always runs upstairs and gets under the desk when I ask if she wants to write a book. (That's her way of saying yes.)

Jon, this book wouldn't be here without your love and support. I'm so lucky to be married to you. Thank you for being there for me every step of the way, every day of my life.

A Note from the Author

I grew up in sunny Southern California with my parents and my two younger brothers, Andy and Jared.

Five days before my eleventh birthday, Andy suddenly died. He was nine years old. We were very close and his loss was devastating.

For me, fiction had always contained the best and realest kinds of answers, so that is where I turned. I sought out every book I could find that dealt with death and grief. I read my favorites—*Charlotte's Web* and *Where the Red Fern Grows*—so many times that I knew entire passages by heart. These books were beyond reassuring to me. They told me that it was okay to feel deeply and that it was okay to be sad. And when I read them, I never felt alone— which, to me, is the entire point of reading, if you want to get right down to it.

I noticed something about these stories. In some, the character died at the very end, after we grew to know and love them. These were the most heart-wrenching. In others, the main character sought healing from a loss that happened before the book began. These showed me it was possible to go on. However, I never felt deeply attached to characters who had died "off the page" before the story started.

Even as an eleven-year-old, I couldn't help but wonder: Exactly how do you get from the fresh devastation of grief to a place where you feel more at peace? Was there a way to write a single story that contained both the initial, acute feelings of loss *and* the transition to resolving those emotions? In other words, I wanted both sides: I wanted the Before and After.

This was my goal for *When Sea Becomes Sky*.

Bex and her parents will always feel the exact shape and weight of missing nine-year-old Davey. But it is my hope that the reader will understand that families continue even after a great loss. Love never ends.

It took me most of my life to figure out how to write this story.

I hope very much that you'll think, like Davey, that it was "worth it."

Thank you for trusting me with your reckless and tender heart.

Jillian McDunn